Professor Odd #12

PROFESSOR ODD
CERBERUS RETIRED

Professor Odd #12

by
GOLDEEN OGAWA

a Heliopause Production

FICTION/Science Fiction, Adventure

FICTION/Fantasy, General

First Edition 2018

ISBN: 978-1-945781-10-0

Prologue

TO AN OUTSIDE OBSERVER, the hijacking of Heliotrans Run 4413—better known as the Cerberus Express—began when it was boarded by a group of aliens who took control of the engines, causing it to stop in the middle of the Denallian Passage. In truth the story began a little before that, when four passengers appeared out of the galley's air lock and proceeded to sit themselves at the front of Coach 20 where they took up an entire row. By their conversation they were quickly determined to be aliens, and a conductor was sent to deal with them. They promptly produced tickets, signed and stamped and perfectly in order—save that they had been issued *after* the exotrain had left Amphitrite, and there was no record of the four strangers having boarded there or anywhere else.

Still, they were perfectly within their rights to be on the train, and the conductor whizzed away after a brisk reminder that they were in coach class, and that their conversation should be kept below forty decibels. One of the strangers—a tall male human with pale skin, short, dark brown hair and eyebrows like a pair of eagle wings—hunched in his seat, looking embarrassed, but his companions—an equally tall humanoid woman with fluffy, cherry-pink hair in a green trench coat, and a pointy-eared anthropomorphic dog with gold fur wearing a navy denim jumpsuit—seemed hardly contrite at all. The fourth member of their band was a barrel-shaped robot, and though its expression was impossible to discern, its reaction to the conductor's request was clearly audible for the entire coach to hear:

"THIS IS NOT A DANGEROUS LEVEL OF NOISE," it began before the dark-haired man shushed it. "IT'S NOT LIKE I SOUND ANY MORE PLEASANT WITH THE VOLUME DOWN," it finished, but only to the ears of those in the nearer rows.

"I believe it is the thought that counts," said the pink-haired woman, stretching comfortably in her seat. "I am sure everyone appreciates the effort, Dave. Don't let it bother you—come on now, you're missing the show."

TALKING TO STRANGERS

Part One:

TALKING TO STRANGERS

ALISTER BANE LET OUT A SIGH OF RELIEF as he watched the small metal orb that served as a conductor whizz into the air lock and then on to the next coach.

It had been strange enough just trying to imagine the train they were on, never mind actually riding in it.

"An *exotrain,* Alister," Professor Odd had said to him, her jaguar eyes sparkling from between strands of pink hair. "It's a *train* that runs through *outer space.* Eighty coaches long, this one's got a triple engine at the front—that's why they call it the *Cerberus* Express—and it's the fastest way to get from Amphitrite to Typhon at sub-light speeds."

"And just how long does that take?" Elo had asked, dryly.

"Eighteen kadents," Professor Odd had replied, then rolled her eyes up, did some internal calculations, and added: "Or, about four years."

"Four *years?*" Alister had gasped. "People sit on a train for *four years?*"

"Most of them spend at least some of it in suspension," Professor Odd said with a shrug. "But everyone gets up for the Denallian Passage, which only takes four *hours* and is the *best thing.* We'll hop on just before it enters the passage, enjoy the show, then hop off again. We can get tickets at Amphitrite—the Premier knows me—and then jump over to the train."

She grinned at them, bright and a little bit manic.

This, Alister had thought, is what happens to you when you live in a place that can open doors anywhere in the multiverse. See that train? That train moving through *outer space?* Wanna ride it, but only for a little while? Have your ship—place, home, *whatever,* (it's called the Oddity for a reason)—just open a portal joined to a door inside the train and *ta-da!* You were there. To be honest, Alister had been surprised when Professor Odd insisted on buying tickets. But after they had been accosted by a conductor barely five minutes after sitting down—and not even a human-shaped conductor; a robot even more unfriendly looking than Dave's panvironment suit!—Alister understood her precaution.

Lightly belted in and hovering over his seat ("They keep the gravity at a minimum, to conserve energy," Odd had explained) Alister had dared to glance at their fellow travelers, trying to gauge the impact their interaction with the conductor had had.

This was difficult. Not everyone on the train was human—or even human-shaped—and for those that were, many were strange colors or had slightly altered facial characteristics. Their expressions were as alien to Alister as were the long-necked, bird-faced people, only even more unsettling for all their familiarity in other respects.

"Technically, *we're* the aliens here," Professor Odd had been explaining. "Humans in general, I mean, not just transuniversal travelers like ourselves. Amphitrite and Typhon are both part of the Aquarian system, you see, which was colonized by the Sollan Commonwealth—that's native humans—about three hundred kadents ago. It's become something of a melting pot, however, since this universe became multiplicity-aware."

"YOU CAN THANK THE DENALLIAN BELT FOR THAT," Dave said.

"How does the Denallian Belt have anything to do with this universe being multiplicity-aware?" Elo asked.

"Just what *is* the Denallian Belt?" Alister chipped in, whispering fiercely. "And . . . does multiplicity-aware mean what I think it means?"

"One question at a time," Professor Odd laughed, then looked elaborately around at their coachmates. The seats had been designed for four to sit abreast, then a narrow aisle, and then four more. They were a little wider and taller than the train seats Alister had ridden in back home—before he'd fallen afoul of the Canary Company and been whisked away to the relative safety of adventures with Professor Odd—but it still made for a packed environment, and some of the other passengers had sensitive-looking ears, and were already glaring at the Professor.

"THEY ALL TIE TOGETHER," Dave told them, his harsh voice muted, but no less abrasive and distinct. "THE DENALLIAN BELT IS A BENIGN PARTICLE FRACTURE IN THE FABRIC OF THIS UNIVERSE, HELD IN BALANCE BETWEEN THE GRAVITATIONAL FIELDS OF THE STAR AQUARIA AND THE GAS GIANT TYPHON. IT FACILITATES TRANSUNIVERSAL TRAVEL WITHOUT THE AID OF ODDITIES OR OTHER METAPHYSICAL TECHNOLOGY. THE IN-EVITABLE RESULT BEING THAT SPECIES FROM ACROSS MANY DIFFERENT UNIVERSES HAVE CONVERGED HERE, RENDERING

THIS UNIVERSE AWARE OF DEFINITE OTHER UNIVERSES—IN OTHER WORDS, AWARE OF THE MULTIPLICITY OF WORLDS, OR *MULTIPLICITY-AWARE. DOES THAT ANSWER YOUR QUESTIONS?*"

"Ye-es," said Elo, nodding slowly. "Thank you, Dave."

"The Denallian Belt is absolutely fascinating," said Professor Odd in an eager wheeze. "I've ridden the Passage at least a dozen times, and I always discover something new. All that aside, I wanted to show *you,* Mr Alister, simply because it is the most brilliant thing."

She pointed as she spoke, and turning to follow her direction, Alister found himself looking out the long, rectangular window that filled the wall nearest to them. Because they were sitting in the front of the car they also had a clear view out a smaller window that faced forward—through which Alister glimpsed a corner of the next coach—and by these windows Alister saw exactly what the Professor meant by "brilliant."

From this distance the starry blackness of outer space was cut across, like an arbitrary sort of horizon, by a band of smoky light that put Alister in mind of long-exposure photographs of the Milky Way. Clots of darkness, like ink suspended in water, drifted across like clouds over a desert. They were lit from behind by a profusion of magenta light, which shot shafts through the inkiness like rays of red sunshine. The red haze itself was pierced by bright points of gold, which came and went in a twinkling dance that left Alister mesmerized.

"Why go through it?" Elo asked in a piercing growl. "Sounds awfully unstable, and if it's a *belt* and not a *sphere* you can easily avoid it."

"Not if it's on the same plane as the planets you're traveling between," Professor Odd said in a patient tone. "Which it is, if you're going from Amphitrite to Typhon. You *can* go around it, yes, if you're in a conventional spaceship which can move above and below the plane of the ecliptic, but the exotrains can't do that. They're infinitely more fuel-efficient—which is why they are so affordable and popular—but part of that comes from running on tracks, and you can't *build* exolines strong enough to support that kind of variation: they've got to be as flat as possible, which means if you're running a line between Amphitrite and Typhon, you've got to go through the Denallian Belt. Which is what makes the Denallian *Passage* so remarkable—they couldn't build a track around it, so they built one *right through it,* using all sorts of clever tricks to manipulate the space-time fluidity, and allowing everyday passengers the chance to observe a truly amazing phenomenon up close. It is *wonderful.*"

"Hold on," said Alister, whose grasp of interplanetary travel, while limited, included the knowledge that planets did not just sit in one place, like an island, and this clashed with a fixed line on which a train could run. "How does the line even *work?* Like, what if Typhon's on the other side of the star? You can't just go in the same direction every time—the planet wouldn't *be* there."

Professor Odd was nodding enthusiastically. "*That's* where four-dimensional thinking comes in handy," she said with a grin. "And orbital resonances. Amphitrite and Typhon are in a two-to-one orbital resonance—that is, Amphitrite orbits the star Aquaria *twice* for every *once* that Typhon goes around. And Typhon's year is *exactly* the same length of time it takes for the

Cerberus Express to travel between the two when their orbits synchronize. So you've got the line, right, which is anchored to Amphitrite on one end—it's moving *with* that planet—until it hits the Denallian Belt, at which point it changes tracks to the Denallian Passage (which is anchored to the belt itself and does *not* orbit the star) and once it gets through *that* it's just in time to get picked up by the Typhon side of the line as that comes around for its half-year. The train spends the second half of its journey traveling on a line anchored to Typhon, and reaches that planet just in time for the return trip to set off for Amphitrite, which then repeats the entire journey in reverse. The *key* is that, thanks to the space-time fluidity of the belt, it takes long enough to go through the Denallian Passage for Typhon's orbit to bring it around, while to the people *inside* it actually goes by much faster. It's a puzzle of moving parts, one which the people of this system solved by turning a disadvantage into an asset. It is really most remarkable. The only difficulty is that the trains have to be kept on a strict schedule, otherwise the pieces don't line up and nasty things can happen. It's never pretty when a train runs out of track, but it's particularly bad when it's a train running through *outer space.*"

Alister nodded, and though he felt like the picture in his head of what Professor Odd had described was a little blurry, he got the idea well enough to try nervously searching what he could see of their way ahead, in the hopes of assuring himself that the Denallian Passage was where it should be, and that the exotrain was not going to run out of track and go careening off into space.

"You can't actually *see* the passage unless you're up in the con," Professor Odd said, seeing him look. "Great view, but it's very tiny and cramped and the people there don't appreciate sudden visitors. Besides, the passage isn't as interesting as the Belt itself, which we can see perfectly well from here."

"Just so long as it's *there,*" said Elo, who was clearly having similar thoughts as Alister.

"THIS RUN IS ON TIME AND SHOULD NOT ENCOUNTER ANY SPLITTING," Dave assured them.

"In fact," said Professor Odd, "we're in the process of shifting at this very moment. Hard to tell, because they've engineered it so well. Remember there's a lot more *space* in space, so it's not like changing tracks with a terrestrial locomotive. It's more like a gradual relay. But you'll know when we get into the belt. You'll start seeing . . . things."

Obediently Alister turned and peered out the window. The wisps of ink and magenta haze looked the same as ever, but had the golden lights *moved?* He watched, fascinated, as the backdrop of ink and haze and light *shifted* around them, and then it was like looking at the cross section of a geode.

There were . . . Alister couldn't help thinking of them as *fractures* in space; places where one part had slipped sideways from another, leaving an angular golden scar. They formed a rough pattern, which was what put him in mind of a geode, he thought, but now he looked, the pattern was constantly changing. Sometimes it was a spiral, other times it was crystalline—all sharp corners—and sometimes it was in smooth waves.

Then his view was washed out by a cold, blue light, which filled all the windows for a moment, and left his eyes stinging.

"First marker!" Professor Odd cried in a restrained voice, but now their fellow passengers were also peering eagerly out their own windows, and no one bothered to chastise her. Once he rubbed the afterimages out of his eyes and could see properly again, Alister realized why.

The crystalline patterns had come alive, bleeding in and out of each other in mad swirls. Then, like clouds shedding off a rising airplane, a whole new vista appeared outside the long, rectangular window.

It was like mountains made of crimson clouds, with blue shadows in their depths, rising in billowy crags as far as Alister could see. At each peak was a shining, golden light, and for as many mountains as appeared right-way up, there were just as many that hung down, like huge stalactites, anchored in the streaks of purple-and-pink clouds that stretched, lazily paralleling the ecliptic. Far away the mountain shapes blurred into heaps of crimson mashed potatoes, their stars stained rosy with distance.

It was breathtakingly beautiful and amazing, and then, climbing out from behind a particularly large mountain, the round curve of a planet hove into view.

"Is that . . . ? Is *that* . . . ?" Alister couldn't bring himself to finish the question.

"A glimpse into another world," Professor Odd said in an excited whisper. "Windows, you know, like what the Oddity sees from the space between."

"But we're *in* a world!" Elo exclaimed. "How is that *possible?*"

"A MORE PERTINENT QUESTION WOULD BE, HOW IS IT *STABLE*?" Dave said, forgetting to lower his volume. A few of the aisle-seated passengers looked around in annoyance.

"They are both *fascinating* questions," Professor Odd said happily.

Outside, the planet was coming fully into view. It looked like a rocky, pock-marked world, dry and yellowish, like an ochre version of Mars. A splotch of white near its top suggested a polar ice cap, and it was ringed with a faint line of black, which bled into the cloudy, red spacescape of the Denallian Passage like the ragged edge of paper in water.

"It's *possible* because of a delicate balance between gravity and escality created by the same orbital resonances that make Heliotrans Run 4413 possible, as well. It's *stable* because . . . well, because it *is.* To be honest even *I* don't know why it doesn't collapse or blow apart—or do both at once—which is one of the reasons I keep coming back. That, and I would like to see a manaflot."

Alister blinked, wondering if his ears had tricked him into thinking the Professor had broken down into gibberish. But then Elo was asking, in clear, enunciated words:

"What is a *mana-flot?*"

At his elbow, Alister could feel Professor Odd vibrating with excitement, and he peeled his eyes away from the amazing sight of a planet eclipsing a star pinned to the top of a cloudy mountain, to find the woman grinning madly at them.

"*Nobody knows,*" she said, sounding positively delighted. "That's literally what they're called: when some Sollan Commonwealth settlers asked a Rikilinni what they were, the fellow replied with '*A'ya Manaflottl,*' which basically means 'blowed if I know,' and it stuck."

"And the Rikilinni?" Alister asked.

For answer Professor Odd pointed with a long, elegant finger to a passenger two rows behind and opposite them. They were tall, even sitting down, with two scaly legs that ended in three-toed, taloned feet. They had a plump body covered in black-and-blue feathers, and a round face with a beaky mouth similarly wreathed in feathers, stuck at the end of a long, thin neck—whose longness and thinness were accentuated by the stacks of metal necklaces that were the creature's only clothing.

"The closest thing Aquaria has to natives," Professor Odd whispered. "But only because they got here first."

The Rikilinni twitched, as if sensing their gaze, and Alister tore his eyes away from the alien to stare out the window some more. The ochre planet had disappeared, but now he could see, faded in the distance, more ragged windows into darkness, and more planets through them. Some of these were small and rocky, others huge and streaked with bands of clouds. Still others were dark and glittered strangely. They were not all lit the same; some of them were visible as full discs, while others were crescents of varying fatness, and still others were only discernible by the ring of illuminated atmosphere around the edges.

Alister stared, feeling his mouth slowly open, as more and more windows came into view. Then they passed through another flash of bright blue, and he squeezed his eyes shut just in time.

"Don't tell me, that was the second marker," he heard Elo say, and when the blue had faded from behind his eyelids, he chanced another look.

Back was the misty, half upside-down landscape of mountains and gold stars, but the only window was a single circle, floating between two opposing peaks. It showed a gibbous blue world, streaked with white clouds, under which brown-and-green continents lurked, like whales under the surface of the ocean. The clouds, though thick around the poles, were thin enough that Alister was able to recognize the landmasses beneath, and he felt a lump rise in his throat as he realized what he was looking at.

Several of the human passengers had also recognized it, and a faint murmur echoed around the carriage.

"Isn't that . . . Earth?" Elo asked in a small voice.

"*An* Earth," Professor Odd said. "No telling which universe it's from, except that it's not far off the temporal median. See, there is India, Africa, your Mediterranean, a bit of Europe . . . "

Alister watched as the window to a version of his homeworld slid by, craning his neck to follow it through the windows of the seats behind him. By the general leaning among the humans aboard, he was not the only one.

They had probably studied maps of Earth, he realized. Seen pictures of their planet of origin in history books—or whatever passed for books here. Which was how Alister had seen his world, to be fair, but he fancied he was probably the only one—outside his companions—who had actually set foot on any of the continents just visible beneath the clouds.

Just as the window was slipping entirely out of sight, Alister thought he saw something bright—like the tail of a shooting star—go streaking across the blue-and-white sphere. But then the window passed outside his field of vision, and he was distracted by a subtle shift in the cloudy landscape ahead.

Where before, the mountainous clouds had been uniformly magenta with blue shadows, now the blueness was spreading, seeping out in a glow of pale aqua that rose like steam from the red peaks. Stars of silver were interspersed with those of gold, and a few of them had broken free from their cloudy peaks to hang in the pink-and-purple mist.

It was utterly enchanting and beautiful, and Alister felt a warm glow of appreciation rising in his chest, forcing out the pangs of lonely homesickness.

Beside him, Professor Odd sighed impatiently. "I *do* hope we see a manaflot," she began, and there was a sickening lurch.

The train didn't stop, and it didn't come off its tracks; it felt more like the whole machine had *shivered,* deep in its metallic bones. All the passengers who were not securely strapped in (including Dave) were shaken off their seats, though Dave stabilized himself immediately with a few careful bursts from his anti-grav plates.

"What was that?" Alister exclaimed, all the pleasant, dreamy feelings jolted out of him.

"*Not* a manaflot," said Professor Odd, unbuckling herself and standing up.

Dave extended one cloth-covered tentacle-arm and pushed himself back against the foot of his seat.

"THAT," he said, loud enough for the whole coach to hear, "IS TROUBLE."

At first it didn't seem like anything had changed. The train continued running, the spacescape kept sliding past, and after a time the passengers settled down again.

All except Professor Odd, who remained standing, her eyes narrowed, gazing intently around the coach, as if the answer were hidden in the metal joints and seals of its walls.

Eventually she frowned and said "Hmm," in the same way doctors did to keep themselves from saying "Uh-oh."

"What's wrong?" asked Elo sharply.

"I'm not sure," said Professor Odd, sounding annoyed. "Something, though. Just . . . wait here a minute. I'm going to see what it is."

"I'll come," said Elo at once, unbuckling herself and leaping over Alister's lap.

Alister hesitated. On the one hand he knew it was best to stick close to Professor Odd. On the other he knew that was also a good way to have your holiday derailed, and he *had* been having a rather good time watching the views of the Denallian Belt.

Dave, it seemed, shared these feelings, and hoisted himself back onto his seat so he could have a better view out the window. That decided him.

"Have fun then," he said, giving the Professor a wry smile.

She patted him firmly on the shoulder, and began making her way down the coach, with Elo at her heel, toward the air lock where they'd left the Oddity's portal. Alister turned back to the view, now dominated by a massive, rocky crescent of a planet, platinum-white and pockmarked with craters. He saw striations in its surface as well, which put him in mind of a grid of roads. Or fracture lines in quartz. He wasn't sure. He tried to distract himself by wondering, but couldn't shake the worry which nagged the back of his mind, and constantly threatened to nag the front of it too, if he didn't concentrate on enjoying the view.

The triple engines of the Cerberus Express bore only a rudimentary resemblance to their terran-bound locomotive namesakes. Specifically built for the Amphitrite-Typhon line, they were huge, bulbous things, with three particle-intake manifolds—tubular contraptions with spiky arms of metal reaching out and forward, the depths of which glowed white-gold—arranged with one on its own, a little ahead of the others, and the remaining two side-by-side a little ways back. Behind each manifold was a small bulge housing the command pods; just large enough, inside all the armor and radiation barriers, for a driver and technician to fit, packed head to toe. Struts of reinforced metal stuck out to either side behind the engines: the con towers which Professor Odd had found so crowded. They also served as communication antennae, though any messages they sent would be a long time finding their recipients while the train remained in the Denallian Belt.

Behind the manifolds, the command pods and the con towers, the body of the triple-engine stretched, rectangular and windowless, housing both the fusion generator that powered the impressive engines and the full complement of drivers, technicians, engineers, and staff. They lived in cramped, close quarters, and for the most part ignored the suspension bunks they were technically required to use for at least one kadent per run.

Because the kind of person who chooses to work and live in a relatively small, fragile place, hurtling through outer space, directly above what is essentially a tiny, well-contained star, tends to be the kind of person who is very keen on keeping that place running smoothly, and taking four-month-long naps while someone *else* takes over your job was never an attractive idea.

So in practice the alpha crew was always active, while the suspension bunks held a skeleton beta crew who could ostensibly be woken up and take over operation of the train in an emergency. It was common knowledge that the beta crew would be pretty terrible at this if there were not enough members of the alpha crew to show them what to do—on a voyage as long as Heliotrans Run 4413 the engines would invariably develop quirks, patched in inventive but non-obvious ways, and routines became more and more elaborate and intricate, until someone just coming out of suspension—no matter how much training they had—would be as lost as a layman.

This was a glaring security flaw, but one which had yet to cause the alpha crew of the Cerberus Express any trouble. They had never needed their beta crew, which consisted of an ever-changing roster of junior technicians, engineers and drivers. Because even the sort of person who chooses to work in a small space above a tiny star hurtling through the solar system often decides that spending eighteen kadents in suspended animation for who-knew how much of their natural lives was a waste of time, and moved on to other, more interesting assignments. The result was that the beta crew would have been mostly useless, while the alpha crew became more and more proficient.

However, even the best crew can fail. Especially if their engine is hit by a capsule-like spaceship that latches onto the side of the reactor case, blasts a hole in the armor, and injects nitrous oxide into the atmospheric processors.

Alarms went off, and a few crew members managed to get masks on, but within minutes all the key areas of the engines were manned by people who were about as capable of operating an exotrain as a Pomeranian.

One affected member, performing as only someone who had spent a lot of time thinking about what they would do in a worst-case scenario could, sent off a boilerplate distress signal and engaged the auto-op, before passing out slumped over the controls.

The few remaining conscious crew members quickly found the source of their problems, and crowded around the breach in a concerned huddle. So when the arc of electricity shot through the aperture it was able to jump from one to the other, before terminating in a protruding lever handle.

The masked bodies—humanoid and exoavian—collapsed on the ground, twitching, and lay still. Smoke from the breach washed over them, obscuring their forms, but not enough to cause trouble for the lithe figure in a tight-fitting exposure suit stepping through the breach and into the engine.

It was joined almost immediately by two larger, bulkier figures, who lumbered forward and locked stabilizing braces around the breach.

"Get the translators working," said the first one, turning their helmeted head toward the larger two. "I want to talk to the passengers."

In the distance an alarm was blaring, and interspersed with it was a melodious, artificial voice that said: *"Class six engine breach. Alpha crew compromised. Waking beta crew . . . "*

"Never mind," said the lithe figure in a sharp, highish, no-nonsense voice. "Let's find the spatial locks. And for the love of god, get this thing *stopped.*"

The mountains had given way to gently rolling hills which put Alister in mind of sweeping ocean waves when the pleasant, white-balanced light that filled the carriage was abruptly replaced by emergency red. In an instant the clean lines of the interior were cast in red-and-black outlines, the passengers turning into surprised shadows, the lights of Dave's suit blazing beside him.

That was all the warning they had before they were suddenly thrown against their restraints, and Alister felt the familiar rising in his stomach as the artificial gravity gave out. He was vaguely aware, somewhere in his jostled mind, that several passengers had gone hurtling through the air and hit the front end of the coach with alarming *thuds.* There was also a synthetic voice, speaking above the blaring alarm that had started up, but both were drowned out by the horrendous screaming that was coming from all around them.

The Cerberus Express, like its terrestrial cousins, had an emergency brake. It did not stop the train all at once—the speeds at which it traveled made this comparable to an ordinary train running into fifty feet of reinforced concrete at sixty miles per hour—but reversed its engines and contrived to decelerate at the highest rate that its engineers had deemed both the train and its passengers could endure.

Even though it was *called* the emergency brake, it really wasn't. In fact, most emergencies would only be made worse by stopping the train. Keeping to the scheduled speed was critical to the success of the run—too fast or too slow, and the train could miss its connection with the Denallian Passage, or the Typhon line. Only when the consequences of *not* stopping were worse than missing a connection was the brake activated. Such as if the train's sensors detected a fault in the line.

In essence, the only thing worse than stopping was running out of line, and the *only* time the former would even be considered was if the latter were unavoidable.

Either way, it meant the train was going to spend more time in space than normal and so it began to implement energy-saving procedures even before it came to a relative stop. So all the lights switched to low-energy red, the gravity was shut off, and the temperature lowered to the minimum necessary to support life.

Had she been present, Professor Odd would have been able to explain all this to a confused and increasingly frightened Alister, but while he and Dave were enduring the rapid deceleration from thousands of miles per minute to functional immobility, she and Elo were encountering their own difficulties.

Namely, the difficulty of trying to reverse the emergency brake from the only place in the engines that was not currently flooded with nitrous oxide, all the while bracing against the inertia that was hurling the occupants of Alister's coach against their restraints, or, if they were unlucky, its walls.

At least, Professor Odd was trying to reverse the brake. Elo was in the Oddity, looking for their respirators.

"I left them on the table!" the Professor called over her shoulder, through the tiny circular hatch that was serving as the Oddity's door.

"That doesn't narrow it down much!" came the strained reply.

Professor Odd shrugged and turned back to the controls. They were for raising and lowering the long-range antennae, but since the emergency brake had to be accessible from every control node on the engine (and some of the coaches), it followed that one *should* be able to turn it *off* from any of those places as well.

Someone, it seemed, had thought this wasn't such a good idea, and Professor Odd kept coming up against security walls and messages requesting confirmation from the Master Con. Which, she knew, was located just behind the three actual engines. Which she also knew was soaked in an atmosphere that even she could not think straight in. Hence the workaround from the communication booth.

Inside the Oddity, Elo gave a frustrated growl. "Hold on," she shouted. "I'll be back in an instant!" And the portal vanished.

Professor Odd waited an instant, and when nothing happened but the train kept braking and the alarms kept blaring, she pursed her lips and turned back to the console, her priorities changed. Now, instead of trying to get the train going again, she worked on flushing the atmosphere.

Somewhere out there, Elo had tried detaching the Oddity from the local universe so she could look for the masks properly, and after finding them she could reopen the portal a split-second later in local time in the Master Con, where, if all had gone well, she would have reversed the emergency brake and switched off all the alarms.

Because nothing had changed, something had got in her way. And if something was bad enough to slow *Elo* down, it was bad enough that Professor Odd could not afford to be trapped in a tiny communications booth.

Agent Parthenon sat in the Master Con, surrounded by shipping and passenger manifests, and regarded the the beta crew critically.

They were not in the con with her—it was only large enough for two or three people, and then only ones who knew each other well—but their pictures were displayed on the banks of circular screens that took up the entire ceiling, and with a swipe of her finger she could bring up their names, ranks, ages, gender designations (the Rikilinni, it turned out, had three different genders, none of which correlated with male or female, and the practice had been adopted by some of the Sollans), and their experience records. She was pleased to see none of them had ever *actually operated* the train.

That was good. They would be frightened. Unsure what to do. People like that were much easier to manage.

Which was to say: they were easier for Agent Parthenon to bully.

"They shouldn't give us any trouble," she said, pushing the files off the screens. "Let me see the passenger manifest."

"Uh . . . " said Caruthers, wedged in the doorway. "There are over *eight hundred* of them . . . "

"So run a scan; see if it raises any flags."

There was the quiet clicking of fingers on buttons as Caruthers did just this. Agent Parthenon relaxed into her seat and began shuffling passenger profiles across her screen as Caruthers sent them over. That was the thing about Caruthers: he was obedient, which was a blessing in a commtech operative. He was also over six feet tall and could double as a bruiser when needed. Which Agent Parthenon needed rather a lot. He was almost as useful as Villafranka—her *actual* bruiser—with his re-markable aptitude for precision sniping and chemical warfare. It meant that Agent Parthenon could do with a two-man team what it took an entire unit of other operatives to accomplish.

Such as commandeer an alien space train and take it in for study.

Behind her, Caruthers let out a low grunt. It was as close as the man got to swearing, and it was like a pin going into the back of Agent Parthenon's neck—a tiny sensation that portended se-rious consequences.

"What?" she said.

"Got a flag," said Caruthers. A pause, then: "Two of them."

"Let me see," said Parthenon.

Two profiles were duly placed on her screens, and the agent felt her breath catch in her throat at the names displayed.

That was all they were. Names. No photos, no homeworlds, no preferred pronouns. But Agent Parthenon didn't need any of that to recognize them.

"Specimens ten-sixteen *and* ten-seventeen," she whispered, her eyes going wide.

"Is *that* who Alister Bane was?" Caruthers asked.

"You didn't hear that," snapped Parthenon. "But do a search for something matching the description of Incongruity M87."

More tapping.

"Not getting anything," said Caruthers, and Parthenon exhaled.

Too soon.

"Wait."

"What?"

"I have . . . something. I don't know. Look at who is traveling *with* ten-sixteen and seventeen . . . "

Agent Parthenon peered at the files as they came up on her screen.

"Marhütz Elo," she said, frowning. "And . . . Dave?"

"Dave's species is listed as robot," supplied Caruthers. "But from the parameters recorded by the conductor, it could just as well be an environment suit. Wasn't Incongruity M87 . . . "

"*Aquatic* . . . " finished Agent Parthenon. She pulled herself out of the captain's seat and squirmed around to look at Caruthers . . .

. . . who wasn't there anymore.

He wasn't there because the doorway wasn't there anymore. To be precise, it looked like the outer corridor had been replaced by a set of carpeted stairs, lit faintly by a confusion of multicolored lights.

A golden, furry paw appeared on the topmost stair.

Agent Parthenon sprang into action. Like all agents trained under Director Carver, she had been thoroughly briefed on what was referred to as The Great Breach—that unfortunate incident in which both Incongruity M87 and two alpha-priority specimens had inexplicably vanished. She had studied the security footage of the strange, anthropomorphic canine, and she knew she had to act quickly.

She barreled up the stairs, pulling her arc taser from its holster, firing almost blindly.

She would have missed, but the gun did its job, and on the second rebound the electric current found its target.

There was an earsplitting shriek, and Agent Parthenon found a pair of canine jaws locked on her gun arm. She looked into furious brown eyes, felt the deadly teeth as faint pressure under her armor, and calmly pressed the trigger again.

That only made the canine bite harder, but when she lost consciousness her jaw slackened, and Agent Parthenon pried the animal off her arm.

Taking a pair of restraints off her belt, Agent Parthenon secured the canine, chipped her, and for want of something more secure, tied her to the back of the captain's chair in the Master Con.

"Caruthers!" Agent Parthenon shouted.

There was no response.

Of *course* there was no response. Ten-sixteen had had portal technology. Whatever was on the other side of the doorway, it wasn't the outer corridor anymore.

After double-checking the restraints on the canine, Agent Parthenon charged her arc taser and began to creep, cautiously, up the carpeted stairs and into the lair of Specimen 1016.

The world went dark. Alister wasn't sure if he fainted or if it was just the emergency lights giving out temporarily. He felt dizzy and sick, like some of his brain had been forced out through his nose.

Someone had unbuckled him and bent him over his knees, and when he tried to straighten up he felt gentle pressure on the back of his neck.

"STAY DOWN," Dave ordered.

Alister stayed down.

"Wha-ah-appen'd?" he asked, thickly.

"OUR TRANSPORT HAS BEEN COMPROMISED."

"S-sorry?"

Behind them a Rikilinni had climbed out of their seat and was pulling blankets out of a hidden compartment in the ceiling. They paused, and out of the corner of his eye Alister saw their raptor-like feet turn toward him. They spoke in a harsh language made up mostly of clicks and a guttural sort of rattle. Alister had no idea what they meant, but he recognized that tone: the creature was frightened. Frightened and *angry*.

"THE TRAIN HAS STOPPED," Dave said—whether in answer to his question or in translation of the Rikilinni Alister wasn't sure.

For a bleary moment Alister wondered why this should be so alarming. A stopped train was no big deal. It just sat on its tracks until whatever was wrong was fixed—worst case scenario people could get out and find other transport.

But they weren't on an ordinary train, he realized with an addled jolt. They were on a train in outer space which had to travel at a set velocity otherwise its tracks didn't line up and . . .

. . . *and* they happened to be in a part of outer space where other space craft couldn't reach them. Deep in the Denal-lian Passage, and help coming along the line from Amphitrite wouldn't reach them any time soon.

Alister felt light-headed and cold, and a moment later real-ized this wasn't his imagination: the temperature *had* dropped, and the gravity had decreased.

The pressure behind his neck vanished—to be replaced with a softer, lighter sensation. Someone had draped a blanket over his shoulder. Or tried to. It was beginning to float away—as indeed was Alister, now he had been unstrapped.

He clutched awkwardly at the blanket and groped for Dave. He felt his ankle grabbed instead, and he relaxed incrementally as his mind slowly came up to full cognizance.

"Where's the Professor?" he asked, his first thought that of escape.

Beside him, Dave made an angry buzzing noise.

"I DO NOT KNOW," the creature replied.

"An' Elo?"

"THE SAME."

Alister let out a long breath.

"So what do we do?"

"GIVE ME TIME," said Dave, and when Alister glanced at him he saw all his lights had dimmed.

Nervous, but confident in Dave's problem-solving abilities, Alister chanced to sit up—the decreased gravity meant his brain was now fully supplied with blood—and looked around at their coach.

The Rikilinni that had spoken earlier was moving down the center aisle, distributing blankets. They had pebbly, gray legs and deep blue feathers that contrasted sharply with their orange-and-gold necklaces. Most of the other passengers were still strapped into their seats and looked even more dazed than Alister felt. He saw a dark-skinned woman with her shiny black hair pulled up in a tight, conical bun, accepting a blanket from the blue Rikilinni, and then falling back against her seat. Her eyes focused on Alister, and he looked away.

The few passengers who hadn't been strapped in when the train stopped were now lying in heaps near the front of the coach, where they floated low to the ground. They were all human, and there was a globby cloud around the whole area. Alister realized with a lurch that it was blood.

He made to stand up—whether to go and see if there was anything he could do or just to see better, he wasn't sure—and nearly sent himself careening up into the ceiling. Only Dave's tentacle-arm, which remained wrapped around his ankle, prevented him from cracking his head open on the bulging lower extremity of the suspension chambers.

These were round, pod-like shapes that lined the ceiling of the coach. Each one had a little window and a digital readout below it, and a light which glowed green, blue, or red. Most of the pods had their lights off—they were empty—a few were blue—their passengers were still in suspension—one had just turned green—its occupant was in the process of waking up— and two were red—something had gone wrong inside.

Alister's eyes had begun to adjust to the harsh red emergency lights. Light from the gold starlike things outside was still pouring in through the windows, and it helped to fill in the black shadows cast by the emergency lamps.

"Let me go," Alister said to Dave, once he'd got a good grip on the handle of his seat. "I want to see if I can help."

"NO," said Dave, and his grip, if anything, got tighter.

"But—" Alister began to protest, and then he stopped and realized Dave was perfectly right.

They were in a much more awkward situation since the Professor and Elo had taken the Oddity's portal off somewhere else, and the least Alister could do was not become separated from Dave. Considering how quickly the situation had deteriorated, the best way to be certain of that was to remain physically connected to him at all times.

And, glancing back, Alister saw that the blue Rikilinni from earlier had worked their way to the front of the coach, where they had been joined by a human in a black jumpsuit. The two barely looked at the motionless figures, but went to the third, who was moaning faintly. There was a conference of clicks and hushed voices, and the injured person said something along the lines of needing to recalibrate.

After a while the human in the jumpsuit stood up and came down the aisle, half walking, half pulling themselves along the backs of the seats. They stopped at each row and asked the passengers something, then moved on. Alister feared that when they reached his row he wouldn't be able to understand them, but the human—who had papery-white skin, flat, straight yellow hair, and appeared perfectly genderless—spoke to him in an accented but understandable form of English.

"Do either of you have first-aid training in bio-synthetics?" they asked, their large, black eyes flicking back and forth between Alister and Dave.

Alister had to shake his head, but Dave let out an uncertain buzz.

The white face turned to him expectantly.

"I HAVE NO OFFICIAL DOCUMENTATION OF EXPERTISE," he said.

The human smiled, thinly. They had a single gem set in the middle of their forehead, which twinkled faintly in the dim red light. Alister couldn't tell if it was a decoration like a nose ring, or a part of their body.

"Neither do we," they said. "But we don't know where to start with cyborns, and fer is badly injured."

For a moment Alister thought that "Fur" was the injured person's name, but then Dave replied, sounding even more annoyed than usual:

"I WILL ATTEMPT TO HELP FIHR," which made the word sound more like "fear." It was only after Dave had made his way to the front of the coach, dragging Alister along by the ankle, and he'd had a chance to listen to the white person talk a little more, that he realized that *fer* and *fihr* were actually second person pronouns, roughly equivalent to *he* and *him* or *she* and *her*—with *fiheren* being equivalent to *his* and *hers*—though

Alister found he had trouble recognizing them as such, since the words were completely foreign to him.

He watched, feeling helpless and useless, as Dave went and sat beside the injured person—cyborn, whatever—and began examining them—*fihr*—with his free arms. The other two passengers had been wrapped in extra blankets and put carefully in a corner. He didn't bother asking if they were all right: it was obvious they were already dead.

The survivor was a human-shaped person with metallic, grayish skin, blank, black eyes, a barcode tattooed above their—*fihren*—right ear, and a stripe of pink lights running down the left side of fihren face. These were dim and flickering ominously when Dave and Alister arrived, and when they—*fer*—spoke, it was a croaking sort of rattle, halfway between a human voice and Dave's own, synthesized one.

Alister found himself floating over a conversation he only half understood, ("I AM GOING TO CYCLE YOUR CORE PROCESSORS," said Dave. "Advise against that," moaned the cyborn. "I'm on the Red Giant Oh Ess." "YOU REQUIRE A FULL SYSTEM RESET. DO YOU WANT MY HELP OR NOT?"), but at least he had a better view down the length of the coach.

All down the rows people were active. A few, like the blue Rikilinni and the white-skinned person, were moving among the passengers, distributing blankets or small breathing masks. Everyone had an air of carefully contained panic, and they kept looking at something over the door at the far end of the carriage. Squinting a little, Alister was able to make out a digital display that showed a series of numbers. These were in two sets: on top was a static 4.500.76, while below was a number that began 0.005.4 and climbed to 0.006.1 in the minute Alister spent watching it.

It was a counter, he realized. Counting up to 4.500.76—whatever that was. His mind helpfully supplied several options, none of them pleasant: it could be the amount of breathable atmosphere they had used; the length of time the heat, light, and gravity could be maintained; or, and this was what Alister rather feared it was, it stood for the amount of time the train could spend still in its tracks before it would miss its connection with the last section of line, and the climbing number was how long they had been stopped.

At 0.007.8 Dave finally managed to convince the cyborn to let him power cycle their—*fihren*—core processors, and after a few moments there was a whir of motors and a small bolt of lightning jumped from Dave's suit to the chest of the cyborn. Their—*fihren*—body convulsed once, and then fer opened fihren eyes and said in a much clearer, almost musical voice: "Wow. It worked."

"CAN YOU RUN DIAGNOSTICS NOW?" Dave asked.

The cyborn took a breath to answer, and the door nearest them—the door that led to the next carriage closer to the engines—burst open, and a large humanoid in a dark, armored suit with a visored helmet strode into the room. Alister saw the gun, saw the burst of white smoke spew from its muzzle, and sucked in a short breath of clear air and held it, before his eyes began to sting as the smoke filled the coach.

Elo came around to the sound of angry beeping drifting down the steps from the Oddity. Her forelegs were twisted up in a cramped position, and there was something that felt like a burn all along her left one. The restraints chafed it painfully, but she bit back the automatic yelp to glare around at her environment in search of her enemy.

She blinked. She was strapped to the main seat in the Master Con, her wrists secured in metal and kevlar manacles, which were in turn linked by way of a thick cord that ran from one to the other and through a supporting strut of the chair on the way.

They were good manacles; strong and tight, and the cord, when she bit it, had the same effect on her mouth as aluminum foil. Not something she wanted to chew through if she could help it. The strut had been well chosen, too; no weakness there she could exploit.

No, she wasn't going anywhere any time soon, unless the person with the key to her manacles came back—which, by the sounds coming from the Oddity, wasn't in the near future either.

All of which would have been disastrous, except that she was *exactly* where she'd been trying to get in the first place. The Master Con and the master controls were, not at her fingertips, but, having the sort of body that bent in half rather easier than a human's, could be reached by her hind paws if she ducked her head just right.

It was slow going, typing on an unfamiliar keyboard when she couldn't see half the screens, with less-than-optimal appendages, but the small beeps and clicks of the train's Master Con were thoroughly drowned out by the noises the Oddity was making—it was sounding truly angry now, and Elo almost pitied the person stuck inside (*almost*)—and no one interrupted her.

There was no way to reverse the emergency brake. They were effectively stopped, and the train required authorization from a ranking officer to get it started again. It was something Elo thought she could have worked around, given full use of her limbs, but as it was she satisfied herself with getting the atmospheric processors working again, cleaning out the nitrous oxide, and as an afterthought cycling all the air in every coach as well. It was energy the train's algorithms didn't want to spend, but after seeing that Coach 20's atmosphere had tripped an alert, she overrode all the warnings (feet jerking roughly), and then lay back against the seat, exhausted.

There was a *ping* from somewhere below her seat—where she could not see—and then, like a muddy fuchsia sun, Professor Odd's wig rose into view. Her face was black with grease and smoke stains and her expression was angrier than Elo had ever seen it.

"*Who did this to you?*" she mouthed.

For answer, Elo jerked her left foot toward the Oddity's door. "Be careful," she hissed. "She's got an arc-taser, and I think she knows who we are."

"Who is *she?*"

Elo snarled, silently. She'd gotten a good whiff of the person, but her scent had been masked by her armor, which smelled mostly of nitrous oxide and hot metal. Still, there were only so many people in the multiverse that she had knowingly pissed off, and she had a hunch as to which group this one belonged to.

"I think," she whispered. "I think she's with that *Canary Company.*"

Professor Odd's face sobered at that, and she looked gravely at the door.

"Right," she said.

Elo thought for a moment that she was going to storm into the Oddity on her own, but instead the Professor went to work untying her. It was even slower going than venting the atmosphere had been, and by the time Elo was free, the noises from the Oddity were horrendous.

"Now what?" asked Elo, wincing as she flexed her forelegs.

Professor Odd turned the broken manacles over in her hands thoughtfully, then put them in the pocket of her coat. "Follow me," she said grimly, heading for the portal at last.

Alister had, when he was fifteen and very bored, timed how long he could hold his breath. He'd lasted almost a minute and a half, but that had been sitting in his room on a rainy Sunday with nothing more exciting than temperamental winds outside.

Clinging to the ceiling of an alien space-train-coach while a large armored person shot at Dave through the stinging white smoke made him need to breathe more, it turned out, and it felt like no time at all before his lungs were burning and his diaphragm was aching. He breathed out as a compromise, trying to at least get rid of some carbon dioxide. That eased the pressure for another couple of seconds, and then Alister's chest wanted to expand. It wanted to expand *now*.

A sharp wind sliced through the coach, blowing him back along the ceiling and taking most of the smoke with it. Alister was so surprised he took a breath before he could see clearly.

The dizziness almost overwhelmed him, before cool, clean air flowed into his lungs and the fog lifted from his eyes.

It revealed a scene in disarray. Passengers were cowering behind their seats or clinging to the ceiling, like Alister, and on the ground near the door, Dave was wrestling with the armored person. He had all ten of his arms out and had managed to wrench the gun out of their hands, and was using it to hit them repeatedly in the neck, all the while keeping their other arm and legs from striking his suit. He was also trying to maneuver himself so that his anti-grav plates were pressed up against the person's chest.

Alister watched in dazed amazement as the flash of blue light went off, at the same time Dave let go of the person's arms, and the two bodies went flying apart in opposite directions.

Dave's suit went sailing through the center of the coach, but the armored person slammed backwards into the side of the doorway, where they went limp.

Dave fired his plates again and went coasting forward, spinning slowly, his arms guiding him over the seat backs or moving confused passengers out of the way. He reached the armored person before they fully recovered, and calmly began ripping chunks off their armor. Their helmet came off with a hiss of pressurized air, and Alister found himself gazing down into a grizzled, craggy face locked in an unpleasant expression.

The man—Alister was pretty sure the person was a man— had bright blue eyes that stood out strikingly from his olive complexion and dark hair. His cheeks were lined and his mouth was thin and his teeth, when he snarled at Dave, were yellow and a little crooked.

Dave curled an arm around the man's neck, and said in his loudest and most abrasive tone:

"TELL ME WHO YOU ARE."

There was silence in the coach now, since all the passengers except for Alister had gone to huddle at the far end—including the injured cyborn, who had been helped along by the blue Rikilinni—so when the man answered his voice was audible for all to hear.

"Villafranka," he said, gone a little red but still sneering at Dave. "Comma, Tony," he went on. "Operative number eight-four-eight, two-zero-six," and his mouth shut with a snap.

"Ask him who he works for," Alister called down from the ceiling, when it became clear that Villafranka wasn't going to say any more.

Dave didn't speak, but spared a couple arms to yank fiercely at the man's chest plate. It came away with an ugly snapping sound and the man winced but still didn't say anything.

Under the armor he was wearing a dark gray jumpsuit made of tough, canvas-like material, and across the chest had been printed a logo: two upper case C's facing away from each other, and under them a three-headed yellow dog, with wings.

"Sorry, didn't I say?" said the man, Villafranka, with an un-pleasant grin. "*Canary Company* Operative, and you're not get-ting away from us this time, M-eighty-seven."

The buzzing was beginning to get to Agent Parthenon. It had started the moment she'd entered 1016's lair, low and insistent in the back of her head. She'd looked around for an insect or perhaps a motor to explain the noise, but eventually she realized that it was coming from the huge banks of screens and colored buttons that took up the near end of the ship. So she'd sat down in one of the jump seats and tried to switch the thing off, but she had been stumped by the controls.

This annoyed her. Agent Parthenon had been trained to quickly pick up many languages and control types, but those of the specimen's lair flummoxed her. They equally flummoxed her multiversal translator, which overheated and shorted out seconds after she'd jacked it into what she thought of as the mainframe. She'd been reduced to looking for the big, obvious lever or red button that would power the thing down. The problem was there were several levers, and many of the buttons were shades of red. Most of them did nothing, though one lever made the buzzing rise to an ear-splitting shriek. She put it back the way it had been at once, and thankfully the noise receded.

It was about that time she noticed that the buttons she had thought were red were now green, blue, or orange. She stared at them in consternation, and as she stared the colors shifted before her eyes.

Color was clearly not how you told the buttons apart. She scrutinized them for any other sign—something carved in their surface, perhaps? She switched her visor to display UV radiation, then infrared, but still saw nothing to indicate a difference in the buttons.

So she left the controls and went over to the huge table, which was laden with artifacts from at least a dozen different universes that she could recognize—and several more that she couldn't. It was stunning. Specimen 1016 looked to be a multiversal pack rat. There was even . . .

Agent Parthenon's gaze lurched to a halt at the sight of Specimen 004, laid casually over a solar-powered orrery from Alt 16. The temporal manipulator that had gone missing at the same time as 1016's inexplicable escape. With trembling hands Agent Parthenon reached out to take it.

Her hands were trembling because the buzzing was giving her a headache. She clenched her teeth, trying to keep her head clear, and that was when everything got knocked sideways.

That was to say, *she* got knocked sideways. Something hit her very hard in the side of the head, and she flew sideways, slamming into a chair and bouncing off the wall. Only her encounter suit saved her from a nasty concussion, and as it was the buzzing intensified to the point where she could barely see straight.

She could see well enough, however, to recognize the golden, furry face snarling down at her.

"I don't think that was *entirely* necessary," said a light, husky voice, and Agent Parthenon wincingly turned her head to see Specimen 1016, wearing a dirty pink wig, standing in the doorway with her hands on her hips.

"She tased me so hard it *burned,*" snapped the canine, viciously knocking Parthenon's head back. She tried to get her hands up to defend herself, only to find them caught and bound in her own cuffs. Then the strange paw-hands were at her throat, and she felt the hiss of seals breaking as her helmet came free, jerking roughly over her head.

The buzzing stopped almost immediately, and Agent Parthenon blinked, breathing fiercely through her nose, and was surprised to discover that the interior of the lair smelled like her grandmother's kitchen—wool carpet and clean linen with an undertone of nutmeg. The clash of senses rendered her temporarily speechless, until she heard Specimen 1016 speak again.

" . . . yes but how are we going to get her to be reasonable *now?*"

When your opponent has the physical advantage, better to play your intellectual strengths. Which Parthenon had plenty of.

"I can be reasonable," she said at once, trying to keep her words clear, even though her head was still spinning.

"*Sure* you can," said the canine, sounding unconvinced.

"Can you tell us what you've done with the alpha crew?" asked Specimen 1016, coming over to the table and picking up Specimen 004. She fiddled with it, and the machine made a plaintive hum. Disabled, Parthenon noted with interest.

"Stassed them," she answered, truthfully enough. "Beta crew easier to manage."

"Yes," said Specimen 1016, her eyes glittering uncannily. "*Why* do you want to manage them? *What* are you doing here?"

Agent Parthenon shrugged as much as she dared. "Collecting samples," she said. Which was true, but she decided not to let Specimen 1016 know that "samples" meant the entire train, or that passengers were expendable.

"Of what?" asked 1016, her tone bright and brittle and hard as steel.

Now some prevarication was in order.

"Fuel and raw materials," said Agent Parthenon. "Can I sit up, please?"

Reluctantly the canine drew back, and Parthenon eased herself into a defensive crouch. Her hands were still securely shackled, but she had full use of her feet, and with a little work she could tease the laser torch out of its hidden compartment at her wrist.

"What for?" asked 1016.

"Clean energy, of course," said Parthenon, and it wasn't even a lie that time. The Company *was* extremely interested in clean, sustainable energy, and the technology behind the engines had looked promising from initial observations. Hence Parthenon and her team being dispatched to collect a sample in the form of the train itself.

The tip of the laser torch was poking into the bottom of her palm. She almost had it.

"How many are on your team?" asked the canine.

Agent Parthenon smiled. She could tell the truth here and they'd never believe her, so she did.

"Two operatives plus myself," she said, as blandly as she could manage. The torch was in her hand, just pointed the wrong way. Parthenon adjusted her feet, to draw attention away from her hands.

The canine scoffed incredulously.

"No," said Specimen 1016 thoughtfully. "She was telling the truth there. That's bad. Elite team. Not concerned with native casualties. *Tsk, tsk, tsk.* And I suppose you saw us on the passenger manifest and thought we'd make a nice addition to your haul. *Really* your company is so . . . "

Agent Parthenon decided she didn't want to wait and hear what Specimen 1016 thought of the Company. Torch in hand she sprang forward, knocking over the canine—who predictably latched onto her leg. She swiped at the grasping paws with the torch, and the canine let go with a yelp. She turned on Specimen 1016, who stepped sideways, leaving the corridor to the stairs and the door into the train open.

"Hold onto something, Elo," she said, and tapped a nearby button, while bracing herself against a monitor.

It was like stepping into a wind tunnel. Agent Parthenon was knocked off her feet and tumbled toward the stairs. She thrust out a hand to stop herself, and found it knocked aside by 1016's foot. When she put out her own foot to steady herself, it slipped down the first stair, and suddenly the gravity seemed to increase. Combined with the wind this was enough to send her stumbling down the stairs and into the Master Con, where the wind stopped abruptly, and gravity returned to the gentle suggestion that it had been on the train.

Because she was *back* on the train, Agent Parthenon realized, and made to fling herself back into 1016's lair—only to find the doorway now led to the access corridor, and Operative Caruthers was standing in it, his shoulders tense.

"*There* you are," he said, the relief evident in his voice. "Villafranka has made contact with Incongruity M87 and Specimen 1017, but they've been giving him some trouble."

Agent Parthenon pursed her lips and pushed her laser torch back into its holster. She'd lost her helmet, but she had a backup respirator in their ship. She could manage.

"Then let's go give *them* some trouble," she said with a bitter snarl.

"WHAT IS YOUR MISSION?" Dave was asking for what felt like the tenth time, and Villafranka was starting to answer, as he always did, "Villafranka comma Tony, Operative number eight-four-eight, one-zero-six . . . " when the whole coach shuddered. The dim red light blacked out entirely and ablative shields went down over the windows, sending the coach into complete darkness.

Alister gripped the latch of the nearest suspension pod, pressing himself back against the ceiling, as the coach erupted with shouts and, a little while later, screams. Dave was blaring, and in the blaring Alister heard words:

"EVACUATE. EVACUATE. *EVACUATE!*"

In the dark, Alister became aware of a dim orange glow pricking out on the wall, forming the shape of a rough circle, with brighter points of light at intervals all around it.

Something hard and round slammed into him.

"EVACUATE!" Dave blared in his ear, and Alister found himself propelled backward toward the far end of the coach. Judging by the softer things that thumped into his back, they were hitting some of the other passengers.

"What's going *on?*" he managed to ask, before the breath was knocked out of him.

"THEY ARE INCISING THE COACH," Dave answered, and behind him Alister glimpsed the ring of orange light, which had intensified and spilled out, like melting metal. Which it was, he realized with a jolt; someone was cutting into the side of the carriage.

Which, considering there was only the inhospitable environment of the Denallian Passage outside, would prove disastrous for anyone remaining in the carriage.

Cool, gray light from the air lock between the coaches flooded inside as someone got the far door open. It was quickly choked by dark bodies, packing in one on top of the other. But even with the gravity virtually nonexistent, Alister realized they could not evacuate all the passengers from their carriage into the following one. Sure enough, the doors closed—on screams of horror—long before Dave and Alister reached them.

Someone—probably the blue Rikilinni, Alister guessed—knew how to manage the air locks, however, and it was hardly four minutes before the door opened again, and another group of passengers crowded out.

Alister and Dave were the last—having been the farthest forward when the evacuation started—and just as Alister extended an arm in relief to pull himself into the air lock, he felt something thin and sharp and hard hit him in the center of his back.

. It was so surprising, and so sudden, that he barely managed an inarticulate gasp, and then cold fingers dug into his sides, and he was yanked violently backward. He made a blind grab for one of Dave's arms—felt one brush his fingertips—then he was whizzing through the air until he slammed into a warm, hard body. An armored hand clapped over his mouth, and he heard Villafranka's rough voice whisper in his ear:

"Not again, ten-seventeen. *Not again!*"

"RELEASE HIM!" Dave blared, and Alister peeked over the hand to see the creature's panvironment suit, its lights ablaze, rushing at them down the carriage. Behind it, the air lock had closed for a second time.

There was a thundering *bang* as the piece of wall within the orange circle exploded into the coach, the force of it knocking Dave into the far wall.

Alister struggled, but Villafranka's grip on him was like iron, and he felt himself pulled toward the ragged circle of bright light beyond the newly created aperture. He heard his captor growl, "Give me atmo, Parthenon! I've got ten-seventeen!" And then something was snapped over his head. Surprised, Alister took a breath, felt dizzy, and then the world slid sideways around him, bleaching white as he was dragged through the hole.

The tiny ship attached to the side of Coach 20 remained long enough for the stranded operative to scramble inside, dragging his catch with him. The ship's air lock slammed closed just as the twining arms of Incongruity M87 reached it, and with a sharp blast it took off, leaving a ragged, gaping hole in the side of the carriage. The Incongruity had to change tactics and grip the sides of the hole to prevent itself being sucked out along with the atmosphere, and the ship powered away from the stricken train, through the boundary of the Passage and into the unstable medium of the Denallian Belt itself.

Behind it, still on the train, Incongruity M87 pulled itself back inside, spewing a collection of jarring noises that formed no words in any language in any universe, but which nonetheless managed to communicate frustration, disappointment, and fury.

* * *

Getting the beta crew out of the suspension quarters, where the Canary Company agent had locked them, was fairly easy. Getting them to get the train going again, wasn't.

"Why don't you calm down and explain to me, in detail, exactly who you are and why you think you should be giving the orders?" said their captain when Professor Odd suggested it would be a good idea to start the train. Soon.

"I'm not giving you any orders," Professor Odd said, with what Elo thought was admirable patience.

The beta captain was a pink, blond-haired man with watery blue eyes and a comfortable belly, which he was currently thrusting in the Professor's direction as if it were a third arm.

"I'm only *suggesting*," Professor Odd went on, "that you get this train started and perform the necessary repairs *en route.* By my calculations you can still make the Typhon line without over-cranking the engines."

"Right," said the beta captain, stroking his shiny, pink chin. "And what makes you such an expert on Heliotrans Run 4413? Fancy yourself an exopilot, do you?"

Professor Odd turned away from the man in exasperation. "How are you doing defrosting the alpha crew?" she asked Elo.

"Coming along," Elo said from her perch in the Master Con. "That agent set all sorts of funny booby traps for whoever tried to wake 'em up. I think I just about got them all—"

A faint vibration went through the floor, spreading to the walls, the ceiling, and settling into a low background hum.

Professor Odd flew to the nearest con center and brought up all the exterior displays she could muster. The tower was yet unmanned, but from the Master Con she could control most of the cameras remotely. The screens showed images of the train, its coaches, and a view from the roof of the caboose.

"That feels like we're *moving*," Elo said.

"We aren't moving," said the beta captain smugly. "Engine's powered down, remember?"

"We're *definitely* moving," said Professor Odd, a thrill in her voice. "Oh, oh *Elo,* we need to fetch Alister and Dave—they'd *love* to see this!"

Elo pushed herself away from the controls and crawled over to peer at the screen. "See what . . . ?" she began, and trailed off into amazed silence.

Behind the last carriage, lying along the pearly, glinting line, was something that, to Elo, looked like a giant, semi-transparent kite. A hard, rocky head sat on top of nebulous, triangular wings that stretched out to either side, while sharp spikes, beaded with blue light, ran in a ridge down the middle, disappearing behind the swell of wings only to appear again as a forked tail that faded into the hazy, magenta distance.

"What is *that?*" she whispered.

Professor Odd turned to her, her jaguar eyes shining.

"I *don't know,*" she said, sounding absolutely delighted.

"Oh bugger all," said the beta captain, who'd been watching as well. "Not another bloody *manaflot!*"

"I rather think you should be thanking them," said Professor Odd primly. "It'll be easier for your to start the engines while the train is in motion—" she broke off suddenly, her good humor evaporating.

Elo didn't have to ask; she had seen exactly what the Professor had. Near the front of the train a coach was belching steam from a ragged hole in its side, and in the center of that hole, spread wide like a starfish, was the tiny form of Dave's panvironment suit.

"I think we've done all we can here," said Professor Odd, pushing herself away from the monitors while Elo was already scrambling for the Oddity. "Good luck, captain, and if you get a chance, thank that manaflot for me." She kicked her way past the bewildered man, nearly colliding with Elo as they reached the portal to the Oddity at the same time.

"If Alister was in that coach—" Elo began.

"Dave wouldn't let that happen," Professor Odd said, sharply, pushing buttons and pulling levers. The Oddity *bonged* plaintively, but the portal obediently shifted, leaving the Master Con behind, and opened abruptly onto the damaged coach—via the same aperture that the Canary Company's ship had created.

There was a rush of wind as the atmosphere of the Oddity flowed in to fill the vacated coach, nearly blowing Dave off his perch. Once it abated, Elo barely had time to unbuckle herself and begin saying "Are you all right?" before Dave was threading his arms into the Oddity and pulling himself inside. His suit fell sideways with a *clang* as soon as he made it through the portal, and to Elo's alarm it began venting steam. He was blaring a single, angry note through his translator, one that Elo couldn't be sure was his equivalent of a scream or simply a malfunction.

"DO NOT ASSIST ME. I AM FUNCTIONAL," he said when she went to tip him upright. Peering beyond him into their old coach, she saw that the place looked thoroughly destroyed. From what she could see of it, all the windows had shuttered, and the only light trickled in from the Oddity. It smelled of burnt metal and alien blood and was, as far as she could tell, deserted.

Then Dave was rolling sideways up the stairs on his tractor treads, helping himself along with his arms. There were scorch marks all over his suit, along with some gashes and dents, and one of his anti-grav plates had got a crack in it. He came to a halt with a whine beside Professor Odd, who was flipping through views of the other coaches on the Oddity's screens.

"THEY TOOK—" Dave began, at the same time Odd said, "Where is—" before they finished together:

"Alister?"

"ALISTER."

Elo felt like her stomach had dropped out of her abdomen. Her hackles went up, and she began to growl instinctively. She didn't have to ask who. She knew, beyond a shadow of a doubt, what Dave was talking about. Something had ripped a hole clean through the coach's wall, and the Canary Company agents had to have come from *somewhere*. *Something* had got them through the natural portals in the Denallian Belt and over to the train.

A small ship, probably. Just big enough for the push there and back again. Hadn't that one agent said something about taking the train for study? She pinned her ears back and strapped herself in again.

"Then let's go *get* him," she snarled. "Can you find their ship?"

"Already done," said Professor Odd, who had disconnected from the train. Now the Oddity was floating freely between universes, its door a blank black slab. That would give them the maximum amount of local time to reopen a portal into the Canary Company ship and grab Alister, which they would need to do before it reached its *own* portal. Elo had never seen the Oddity's portals dragged through another portal, but from what Professor Odd had said, it was apparently a very bad thing.

"THEY ARE MOVING EXCEPTIONALLY FAST," Dave remarked, pulling himself upright to get a better look at the screens.

Elo could see what he was talking about now: there was the little ship—hardly more than a pod with some rockets attached—and they were firing on all thrusters toward a ragged, black hole through which the crescent face of a familiar blue-and-white planet could be seen. Pulling back the view Elo quickly saw why:

Another manaflot was chasing them, and from this angle Elo could better see how its rocky, solid-looking head was really more of a skull. Or perhaps a helmet. It sat on top of the transparent, ghost-like body, glowing from within, its huge jaw gaping wide. At least, she thought that was its jaw. Though the creature was symmetrical, and she wasn't certain whether the apertures in the skull/helmet were eyes or mouths or something else entirely.

It was undulating through the medium of the Belt, the blue lights flashing along its spine, leaving a trail of fire in its wake, and no matter how alien it was, Elo could recognize that behavior.

"I think I know what the manaflot are," she said, hollowly. "They're the . . . they're the real natives of Aquaria."

"MUCH ASSISTANCE THEY ARE BEING NOW," Dave said.

"Actually—" Elo began, meaning to tell him about the man-aflot that was currently pushing the exotrain out of its dead stop, but then Professor Odd began hissing like an angry pot.

"A block! An *effective* block!" she practically shrieked. She tore at her hair, which promptly came off and flew across the room to land on the table. Beneath it, her tentacle was coiled tightly, the pale tip writhing around itself in agitation.

"You can't get into their ship?" Elo barked. "Let me try . . . "

She tried, but to no avail. The little ship was battened down tighter than a diving bell. There wasn't even a square inch they could use to anchor the Oddity's portal.

"We could try it unanchored—" Elo began, but Professor Odd had pushed back from the controls, folded her arms, and was staring grimly at the screens.

"No," she said, after a long moment. "I know where they are going. We'll meet them on the *other* side."

Alister slammed into consciousness at about the same time the ship carrying him slammed into something solid. At least, it *felt* solid to Alister, but he seemed to be feeling everything in extremes at the moment. His clothes were too coarse and itchy; the air on his face was stingingly cold and dry, and whatever drug he'd inhaled was making his head pound like the pistons of a steam locomotive.

"You're coming in too steep!" a man's voice shouted. It sounded crackly, as though it were coming through a radio.

"No choice!" shouted a woman, much nearer to him and in person. Her voice cut through the fog in Alister's head like a knife, disrupting the piston engines, and he winced. "Have the retrieval team waiting at these coordinates—Parthenon out!"

After that the world went shaky and sickly yellow around the edges. Alister felt bile rise in his throat, but either he had already vomited or his stomach was otherwise empty, because nothing more came up. He didn't exactly pass out, but he lost time in clumps.

He was in a small space with his hands twisted behind his back and straps holding him to a stiff board. He was sideways, or upside-down, or standing on his toes. There were lights flashing everywhere, the shadows of three hunched bodies nearby.

There was fire all around them outside. It felt like his insides were floating upward into his chest. He was weightless again.

Then there was darkness, and the gravity was crushing. Something bubbled up in his agonized mind and came out as a sort of groan.

There was a *phuzzzzzzzt* of radio static, and then the woman from before said: "This is Agent Parthenon, the duck is in the water and we're all alive. Negative on the exotrain, but we recovered a specimen. No, you don't have clearance for that. Get the retrieval team here, now."

The roof came off the little black world Alister and his captors had been stuck in, and people in masked hazmat suits crowded around the rim. Black-gloved hands unfastened (but did not untie) him, and he was lifted clear of a tiny spaceship, its ablation plate burned away to almost nothing, while around him bobbed the bloated gray forms of life rafts. Beyond that was blue. A dark blue ocean and a pale blue sky, and in his nostrils the smell of salt and burned metal.

"Prep him for transport," the woman was saying. She had bronzy skin and thick black hair pulled back into a tight bun, and she was wearing a suit of close-fitting armor. She also had a headset microphone and a collar with the double C's and three-headed, winged dog of the Canary Company. "He's had recent contact with Incongruity M87. He needs to be quarantined at HQ."

The open air of the ocean was rushing into him, lifting away the last traces of the drug. The gentle rocking of the waves was soothing after that hellish ride, and Alister found his mind was clearing rapidly. With the lifting of his mental fog, there was no panic beneath. Instead, Alister found only a dull resignation.

They had got him. After countless worlds and who knew how many years, he was right back where he'd started with Professor Odd—in the hands of the Canary Company. It seemed, now he thought about it, an inevitability. It was something he'd spent so long worrying about happening that, now it was actually happening, it was almost a relief: the waiting, at least, was over.

Now on to the next bit.

As he was lifted into a hammock to be pulled up to a waiting helicopter, he found himself briefly at eye level with the black-haired woman.

"You won't keep me, you know," he said, his voice almost lost in the chop of the helicopter. "She'll come. She might already be here."

The woman met his gaze, and Alister was astonished to see outright hatred in her face. Then she smiled. It was a small, satisfied smile, and it frightened Alister more than anything he'd seen that day.

They pulled him up into the helicopter. There was another hellish ride, and then someone put a black bag over his head and he lost track of space.

The helicopter landed. He was pulled out, put on what felt like a gurney, and wheeled to another vehicle. Probably a van, just like last time. They drove him for a while, and eventually he was unloaded into a place that smelled of antiseptic. He was put in a small cell with a thin blanket and a hard pillow, and finally given use of his hands. When he pulled the hood off and looked around he found it was dark—the only aperture being a barred window with a metal grate behind it, shut fast.

Alister leaned back against the wall and waited. Professor Odd had come for him in far, far worse places. It was only a matter of time.

Alister waited there, in the dark, listening to nothing but the ringing of his own ears, for a very, very long time.

No one came.

Professor Odd had found the universe in a matter of seconds. Had found the entry point of the Canary Company ship in just a few more. She'd located the door nearest to the cell where they'd taken Alister, and was just about to drop the portal when Elo let out an inarticulate bark, leapt across the aisle, and yanked the Professor's hands off the keyboard.

"*Stop,*" she managed to gasp, in English, at last. Her paws were shaking.

"Elo? Elo, what is it?" Professor Odd's body was a rigid frame, her hands frozen with her fingers splayed over the keys.

"*Look,*" wheezed Elo. "*Look* at the temporal lock!"

Professor Odd looked—the time at which they would enter the universe was displayed in a series of blinking lights near one of the lower screens, at first glance no different from all the other blinking lights—"But I set it to . . . " she stopped. She looked again. Her eyes bulged.

With a few taps at the rack of buttons she released the universe and tried again. She set the temporal lock, with the utmost care, at the exact same moment as Alister's entry point. But when the Oddity tried to connect with the universe, the lock broke and the time of entry slid forward. A *lot* forward. Had she opened the portal, they would have come through almost a *year after* Alister arrived.

"No," whispered the Professor, and tried again—this time pushing the Oddity's portal even further back; three hours before Alister's arrival, which was as far as it would go.

The same thing happened. It jumped to a day in June, ten months after the pod from the Canary Company went through.

Elo was growling, deep in her throat, without realizing it.

"That agent," she said through the snarls. "She *did* something when she was in here!"

"It could be a natural temporal incongruity," Professor Odd said, but she did not seem convinced. "Or, they could be doing something from their end." She stroked a tube of light that ran up from the floor nearby. "The Oddity was blocking that agent. She couldn't have known what she was doing." She let her hand fall, her shoulders slumping with it. "I don't know *what* they know. They've had access to multiple universes, and there *are* things that can mess with the Oddity's doors. If they got hold of a portal destabilizer that might do the trick . . . " she trailed off.

Elo felt ready to crawl out of her skin. Her forearm was still hurting, she was beginning to feel sick with worry about Alister, and the Professor was just *sitting* there. She wanted to bite something, but instead she went back over to her own seat and tried to get a peek at what was happening to Alister. But though the monitors could track his progress through the universe's space-time continuum, the information was of only the vaguest and most rudimentary kind.

There was a sloshing sound from the kitchen alcove. Dave, who'd parked his panvironment suit there and fairly writhed into the sink once he'd got the water going, blinked at them over the porcelain lip, his eye rising like a pinwheel orange-and-yellow sun. Then, slowly and deliberately, he crawled out of the sink and over the carpeted floor toward the Professor. He left a trail of water and slime in his wake, but Elo hadn't the heart to complain about it.

Dave reached the Professor and plucked at her coattails. The woman broke off frowning at the Oddity's controls and obligingly leaned over so Dave could crawl up onto her bare head, his green, octopus-like arms draping gently over her shoulders. One of them, trailing down her back, found her own tentacle, wound tightly at the base of her skull, and gently pried it open. In response, the Professor's tentacle wrapped around the arm like a creeping vine finding a hold on a tree branch.

Despite the invertebrate nature of the appendages, Elo recognized the gesture as a comforting one, and not for the first time she wondered how much of Dave's personality was lost in his monotone translator.

They stayed that way for some time; Professor Odd hunched over the controls with Dave wrapped around her head, speaking in a language that could not be heard save via the transmission of his psychoactive slime. They didn't communicate this way very often, because of the mess, and Dave never tried it with Elo or Alister. They had both heard his true voice, however, on the one occasion when he had to extricate their minds from a simulated reality. The memory of it brought a shiver down Elo's spine, and though she was dying to know what was being said, it was not enough to make her go over and stick her head under Dave's mantle.

Eventually the Professor's shoulders gave a little shake, and she sat up straight. One of Dave's arms had slipped, so it covered half her face, but her visible eye found Elo, and its gaze was steady and direct.

"Leave off that universe," Professor Odd said. She paused, spat out some slime, and went on. "We're not getting in *that* way."

"There is *another* way?" Elo asked incredulously. She had entertained the possibility of visiting some other universes first, to see if that jogged the temporal slip, but that was as likely to make it slip the *wrong* way as anything else.

Professor Odd blinked her single, visible eye, and a drop of greenish slime ran down the side of her nose. "There are lots of different ways," she said. "I just can't access them."

"So what good does that—" Elo began, but the Professor had held up a finger for silence, and she snapped her mouth shut.

"*I* can't access them," she repeated. "Well, I mean, *some* of them yes, but what would be the point? I stay with the Oddity; it's as simple as that. But there *are* other ways of getting between universes—as the system of Aquaria and our friends at the Canary Company have shown—and more importantly there are *other* people who can go places *I* can't. Namely," she rolled her eye upwards.

"Dave?" asked Elo, hardly daring to believe.

"How do you think he got into Alister's world in the first place? Walking? No, Dave here can jump worlds, given the right circumstances. He just can't take his panvironment suit with him. So, he'll go on ahead and we'll meet him there. And in the *meantime*," she went on, before Elo could point out the riskiness of such a plan. "In the meantime, we're going to find him some *backup.*"

The right circumstances for Dave to get into Alister's home universe turned out to be a lake under a stormy sky on a planet whose atmosphere even Professor Odd couldn't breathe. They opened the portal just long enough for Dave to writhe out through a natural gateway formed by a jumble of rocks, over the wet beach, and to watch him disappear beneath the surface of the blackish water. Then the Professor switched the portal off and spent a long time staring at the glowing, colorful buttons of the Oddity's control panel.

Elo came over and stood at her shoulder, internally quivering with nerves while trying outwardly to remain stoic and calm.

"The rats will understand," Professor Odd said, after what felt like an eternity. "They will help. And the dogs—yes, the *dogs*—they might be willing. And of course . . . there is always *him.*"

"Rats?" said Elo. "Dogs? Who's *him?*"

Professor Odd looked up, as if only just now realizing she was not alone.

"Elo," she said, her eyes very earnest and clear. "Apart from me and Dave, you know more about interdimensional travel than anyone I've ever met."

Elo sniffed. "Because I learned from *you,*" she said.

Professor Odd shrugged off the implied compliment. "Point is, getting between universes without the Oddity can be a little tricky. Even if your world has the way, doesn't necessarily mean travel is feasible. Would you be able to—I mean, if you had a willing team—do you think you could . . . "

"Give the natives a helping paw?" Elo finished, feeling her panic and frustration condensing, solidifying into a hard ball of grim determination, high in her chest. A solo mission, effectively, away from the relative safety of the Professor and the Oddity. But for the Professor—for *Alister*—she would do it. She didn't bother being surprised at the intensity of the feelings of protectiveness and responsibility that rose up in her when she thought of him. Alister had entered her territory like an abandoned puppy, and since then had become an important member of her pack. It was a small, unconventional pack, but Elo protected its members with a tenacity that would have done justice to her feral ancestors. She found herself grinning in the human manner, which she knew most people found unsettling, but then, this was hardly something to smile about.

"Tell me what you need me to do," she said.

Professor Odd beamed at her, briefly, like a flash of sun glancing off a mirror. "In just a moment. We should get the rats on it first, since they're closest."

Elo frowned. "What *rats?*"

Professor Odd smiled, tightly, and began recalibrating the portal. To Elo's surprise, she saw they were going back to the same universe with the exotrain and the Denallian Belt. Same solar system, too, but instead of latching onto the train, Professor Odd had the portal open into a space station orbiting a bright blue gas giant. Elo caught a glimpse of it out of a huge observation window that filled one side of the promenade of gracefully curving arches of silver steel, with little pearly lights strung along their length. Small, bright ships moved between them, and beyond the blue swell of the planet she could just make out other space stations, falling in orbit with them.

"Is that . . . isn't that *Amphitrite?*" she asked, following the Professor out onto the promenade—which had a floor of polished black stone and a number of people—human and Rikilinni—in the distance. Which distance was disappearing rapidly as they spotted Elo and Professor Odd, and began rushing in their direction.

"The very same," said Professor Odd, turning and striding toward the approaching group with fearless confidence. "I told you the Premier owed me a favor. Well, several favors. A perpetual favor, you could say. Did I ever tell you *why?*"

"Not that I recall," Elo said, dryly.

"I really should," said the Professor. "After this is over. Marvelous story, really. Good dinner conversation. But the short version is this: I saved her life. Her life, and the lives of some other, *extraordinary* people. Ah, hello my distinguished individuals!"

This to the group of people who had at last come within hailing distance. They were a motley bunch: a human man, two Rikilinni and a white-skinned cyborn of indeterminate gender. They were all wearing what was recognizably a uniform: blue tops with high, stiff collars, and an emblem embroidered on the sleeve. The humanoids carried low-profile pistols, while the Rikilinni had mean little batons under their stubby arms, but the weapons remained in their respective holsters as they came to a disorganized halt at the Professor's words.

"I'm glad to see you still recognize me," Professor Odd said— and without her dark glasses and wig, it would have been hard not to, Elo thought. "Not to sound cliché, but I do mean this literally: *Take me to your leader.*"

This was done, amazingly, with no protest whatsoever— though Elo caught the cyborn giving Professor Odd astonished looks, and whispering to the human in words they thought were inaudible, but which Elo's keen ears picked out easily:

"That's the—I mean, that's *the*—"

"Yes," said the man through gritted teeth.

"She actually *exists!*"

"Of course she does, now *shut up,* the wolf can hear you."

Both of them glanced at Elo at that, who, despite their desperate circumstances, couldn't help giving them a toothy grin.

They were led out of the promenade and into a roomy elevator which carried them deeper into the space station, through several thick doors that opened with hisses of pressurized air, and finally into a circular room richly furnished with wooden chairs and tables, which were in turn covered by embroidered cloths or thick, woven rugs. The place smelled of wool and wood polish, and reminded Elo of the contents of a Victorian sitting room from Earth transferred to an advanced space ship.

Which might very well have been exactly what it was.

At the center of the room was a huge wooden desk, covered with little stands holding transparent tablets aglow with words and figures. Behind the desk sat a hooded figure, their back to them, looking up at a wall full of monitors. These displayed a block of code that even Elo couldn't read, but whatever it was must have been important, for the figure didn't turn around until after the big, reddish Rikilinni—who seemed to be the one in charge—had coughed twice and said something in their clicking language.

Elo caught a whiff of something both alien and familiar and definitely *not* human, and that was all the warning she had before the figure turned around, and she found herself looking up into the long, pointed, pink-nosed, black-eyed face of a giant anthropomorphic rat.

Her fur was a rich, honeyed brown, and there was a subtle twist to her mouth and around her eyes that suggested a human spectrum of emotions and thoughts lay behind the murine façade. She looked at Professor Odd, twitched her nose, and with a motion of one pink, and undeniably *human* hand, sent their escort hurrying from the room.

"What's gone wrong *now?*" asked the rat-person. She had a raspy, gruff voice. Elo thought she detected an Anthropocene Earth Spanish accent, but it might have been something else. "You only ever visit when something's gone *wrong.*"

"Not true!" said Professor Odd. "I came here for dinner, once. Just for fun. Ask Kaklee."

"I *know,*" said the rat-person, who Elo assumed was the Premier of Amphitrite. "And you didn't even stop to say *hello*—"

"There were *children* involved!" Professor Odd protested.

Elo coughed, causing the Premier to glare at her. It sobered the Professor, however, who clasped her hands behind her back, and went on, almost contritely.

"The fact is," she said. "And I *am* sorry about it. But the fact is, there is trouble. A lot of it. You'll want to get a message to the Premier of Typhon as soon as you can—the Cerberus Express encountered some problems in the Denallian Belt, and the beta crew was in charge when I left."

"The *beta* crew—" the Premier began, pulling down her hood so she could train both her round ears at the Professor. "Why did you *leave?*"

"*Because,*" said the Professor, and took a deep breath. "A friend of mine was kidnapped, and he's in even more danger than the exotrain. The people who took him are the bad sort of scientists, more interested in invading other universes and stealing their technology—and inhabitants—than in actually *learning* how the multiverse works. I'm going to rescue him, but I need help. I need the Rats of Alnitak."

The Premier's whiskers twitched, and she seemed to expand a little. "Give me the coordinates—for your friend *and* the exotrain," she said briskly. "Come back in a week to debrief the kids."

"You can count on it," said Professor Odd, and leaned over the desk to embrace the rat-person.

"A *week?*" asked Elo, while they were being led back to the promenade.

"We have time," said Professor Odd. "As long as I don't try to enter Alister's world, it doesn't much matter what I do beforehand. Now it's time to find *you* a team, I think."

"I think," said Elo, who'd been doing some considering in the Premier's office. "I think I know exactly where we should go next."

The huge power poles marched away across the windswept, gray-green plain. Drooping from their arms in graceful arcs were strands of thin cables, hardly visible in places against the bright sky packed with white clouds. They ended in a city of towers and metal boxes, built on a concrete platform which also supported domes of shiny, blue-black stone. A big black sign with white pictograms warned all approaching that dogs would be struck by lightning if they did not wear proper protective gear.

The tall, silver-and-cream dog with a face like a knife looked over at the conversion plant from where she sat in the little garden outside the bunker, sipping her afternoon broth. It wasn't that she *liked* looking at the conversion plant, it was just that it was the only thing *to* look at when you worked at NeoCanii Base North. Well, if you didn't want to bust your eyes watching computer screens all day.

And then, very suddenly, there *was* something else to look at. Someone had come out of one of the access doors on the side of the largest conversion box—a door which the dog knew led to a solid bank of wires and circuits—and they were assuredly *not* wearing proper protective gear: they were covered from ears to tail in a bulky suit laid heavy with bags and packs and the sharp, angular shapes of weapons.

The dog straightened up and watched in amazement as the person then *dropped to all fours* and loped through the conversion plant, scaled the chain-link fence surrounding it, dropped to the ground on the other side, and then continued loping straight for the base.

The dog's broth had gone cold in her paws. She stood and stared as the figure, having spotted her, altered course and made for the little back garden outside the bunker. When it reached the low stone wall that separated the carefully tended plants from the rough grass outside, the figure stood up, and the dog was astonished to see an intelligent yet *feral* face staring at her from amidst a swirl of rich, golden fur.

Memories of half-believed stories and unbelievable mission reports swelled up inside the dog's head, and she fumbled in her coat for her regulation comsys. She hardly needed it nowadays, but she couldn't know that this dog—wolf—*canine*—spoke their language.

Then the person spoke, both in audible Standard and in a form of *canilingua* that the dog could just about understand. They said:

"Is that you, Ksarios?"

The dog flicked both ears backward, then forward. *No.* Then she got her comsys turned on—its damn batteries were low again—and speaking as carefully as she could in both languages, answered:

"I am Natalyas, her daughter. Are you . . . are you the *golden wolf?*"

The stranger's face made an expression of mixed amusement and disgust. "I am no wolf," she said. "I am Marhütz Elo of the Black Thirteen Auxiliary, a *vroknaär* of Aratowan, and I have a mission for you."

And now, a conversation that may or may not have been recorded. Due to the specific circumstances surrounding it, aside from the two participants, no one else would have been able to hear it, taking place as it did across the void between universes, packaged in time and light and the motions of atoms.

But if someone had the power to unravel the code and sort the messages into the correct order, it would have sounded like this:

"Hallo?

"I know you're out there.

"I know you're listening.

"I tried contacting you before, and it didn't work. *This* is working now, I can tell. So why don't you answer?

"Are you cross with me? I hope you're not. I took care of some people who needed help. They were looking for *you*, but they got *me* instead. I think I managed to help them rather well. Just thought that, in the broad scheme of the multiverse, you might be willing to . . . er . . . well, take a call for *me* as it were. Now. Because I can't."

"You are referring to the Antimovian incursion on Primo Terra BK thirty-eight seven?"

"Oh great hitch you've given them *numbers?* How dull. But yes, yes that would be the one."

"I've just come from there. You should know you left that world vulnerable to future incursions and some rather impertinent people took advantage. I was put to extreme inconvenience sorting it all out."

"Sorry about that."

"Yes"—a contrite cough—"I did appreciate the gesture."

"Those *impertinent people,* they didn't have multiversal technology and wear an emblem sort of like two Cs and a winged dog?"

"How could you possibly know that?"

"Because *I've* just come from a world where they were being *very* impertinent."

"Oh?"

"They tried to steal an exotrain."

"My dear, surely you jest."

"Don't you 'my dear' me, I'm not your Irene Adler."

"A multitude of apologies, Professor."

"Yes, well, anyway. That's not the worst of it. I got them off the train—well, I think mostly the manaflot did that *but*—the real problem is . . . they have my friend. You remember Mister Bane?"

"How could I forget?"

"They took him."

"What on all the earths could they want with *him?* Not that he didn't seem a nice, stalwart lad, perhaps a bit *plain* . . . "

"They belong to *his* native universe! He got mixed up with them entirely by accident, all because of me—well, me and Dave, *but*—for some reason they think he's got some special, secret knowledge of how the multiverse works, and I took him *away* from that world to keep him safe from them."

"And now that they have reacquired him, you fear for his well being?"

"Yes."

"And now he actually *does* have some valuable knowledge pertaining to the workings of the multiverse."

"Yes."

"And I assume, since you are asking *me*, that for some reason your . . . *usual* means of transport has been compromised?"

"Pretty much exactly right, yes. Look, I'll give you the whole rundown if you'll agree to help."

"And why would I do that, my dear Professor?"

"I'll even let you call me your 'dear,' see? I'm *hoping* you'll help because you are, against all first impressions, a *decent person,* and that you actually do *like* helping people. Also, I think you dislike the Canary Company even more than I do—which is saying something!"

A silence filled the empty space, and anyone piecing together the conversation might have been fooled into thinking it stopped there. But a little time later the second voice—which was smooth and rich with an educated accent—came back.

"Meet me on Primo Terra FJ seventy—it's the one with the Icelandic Empire, you can't miss it—and wear a hat, it's cold in Reykjavík."

"*Where* in Reykjavík?"

"It doesn't matter. I will find you."

And after that there really was silence. It stretched on forever through the void, eating up the unheard conversation, until there was no trace of it left whatsoever.

The Oddity's lights were dim, and the darkness which usually hovered high under the ceiling stretched down and curled in the corners of the place like a black fog. It draped over the table and hung around the shoulders of the thin figure sitting at the controls. She sat very still, her back ramrod straight, and her olive-green trench coat fell in stiff folds around her legs. Her long, pale hands rested on the bank of colored buttons, their rainbow of lights reflected in her brown, feline eyes. She blinked once, causing the reflections to die and be reborn in between the swipe of her thin, platinum lashes. She wore a thick wool scarf wrapped around her neck, and a wig with cream-colored hair tipped in pink sat on her head. In the depths of the Oddity, the place hummed in soft anticipation.

A shift and a whisper of fabric announced movement: Professor Odd had reached into her pocket and removed a crumpled piece of paper. Spreading it open over the buttons, she ran a finger down the bulleted list of items, each of which had been marked off with a neat red tick.

When she had been down the list twice, making doubly sure each item had been accomplished, at last she stood up—pushing the list back into her pocket—and turned toward the door.

It was a matte, black rectangle, but with the swipe of a lever the Oddity *bonged,* and the door changed to a plain metal affair with a round handle in the center.

Professor Odd clenched and unclenched her fists, inhaled to the deepest extent of her lungs, and then let the air out in a long, measured breath.

She walked down the steps, grasped the handle firmly, and pulled the door open.

Clear, white-balanced light flooded onto the stairs of the Oddity; the portal led to a long hallway with a neat, linoleum floor and square lights bolted to the ceiling. There were no other doors.

Professor Odd walked down the hallway, her shoes making soft *clicking* noises on the clean floor. The place smelled faintly of cherry blossoms, making her wrinkle her nose.

At the end of the hall she consulted the map that had been nailed to the wall, and after a moment turned left, went up a flight of stairs—which had once been corrugated metal but were now covered with carpet—and then along another hall, this one with windows that looked out onto a central courtyard where there were fruit trees in bloom. Several of the windows were open, letting in wafts of fragrant air.

Professor Odd walked faster. The hall here was carpeted as well, so she moved in utter silence up to the big door with a frosted glass window.

The frosted glass had once had an emblem etched onto its surface, but this had been scratched out of existence and a sticker of a bird put in its place. Professor Odd frowned at it for several seconds, and then for several more where, on the wooden plaque below the window, someone had painted over the name that should have gone there, so it only said: "DIREC-TOR ---------"

Professor Odd pursed her lips, took firm hold of the door's handle, and went inside.

The room beyond was clearly the deputy office—there was another door on the far wall with "AUTHORIZED PERSONNEL ONLY" stenciled over the scratched-out logo—and it was filled with bookshelves and one man-high computer. A small desk was squeezed between these, and behind it sat a small, plump woman with coppery skin, slanted eyes, and black, frizzy hair. She stood up in surprise at seeing Professor Odd, her dark eyes going round in amazement.

"Director," she said, her voice high with nerves but otherwise pleasantly musical. "*Director,* you need to get out here *now!* It's *her!* I'm *sure* of it!"

Before Professor Odd could even open her mouth to respond, the door on the far side of the room slammed open and a man leapt out.

He was a tallish man, narrow in the way tall people are without really being thin, with dark brown eyes and dark brown hair that had been shaved back to a short fuzz all over his head. As if to make up for this, he had acquired a thick, full beard, neatly trimmed, which almost completely hid the lines of worry that had been seared onto that face since the last time Professor Odd had seen it. He was wearing a somber brown blazer jacket and trousers, but the shirt peeking through at his collar was a garish combination of orange-and-pink swirls that stood out like a poppy in a muddy field.

"*Professor!*" he cried, trilling both his Rs in excitement. "You're *back!* You're *here! Finally!* We've been looking all *over* for you! Even *Elo* was getting worried!"

He'd reached the woman's desk now, which stood in his way of advancing any farther unless he wanted to go around a blockade of bookcases. He got around this problem by stepping up onto the desk—the woman snatched a metal tablet from under his patent leather soles—and hopping down on the other side. Spreading his lanky arms wide he threw them around the Professor's shoulders and embraced her briefly, before pushing himself back—but not letting go of her shoulders—to grin at her.

Professor Odd blinked, her wide eyes going impossibly wider as she stared at the man in amazement and consternation.

"Mister *Alister,*" she whispered. "What on all the earths has *happened?*"

Alister Bane giggled at that. A happy, bubbling sound quite at odds with his formidable appearance. His swooping eyebrows wiggled at the ends as he shrugged.

"Who'd have thought *I'd* ever be *answering* that question?" he said, and then sobered up. He cleared his throat. "You're late, Professor. Almost two years late, by our best estimate. You can blame Dave, if you like, but I wouldn't. He was going to fix the interference they were running, but then . . . well, he never got around to it. Anyway, you're here now, which is the important thing. Raji, Raji," he said, half turning to the woman behind the desk. "Can you get a message through to Elo? Tell her the Professor has turned up at last!"

"I can try," said the woman, who was still staring at Professor Odd like she was a character out of a storybook come to life. "Might take a while to reach her, though."

"Better send it right away then," said Alister, and turned back to the Professor, still grinning hugely.

At last Professor Odd raised her own hands and clapped Alister on the shoulders.

"My reinforcements came through? You got my message?" she asked.

"Oh yes," said Alister, stifling another laugh. "Did they *ever.*"

Professor Odd's grip tightened a little, then she released him.

"Tell me," she said, pinning him with an intense, catlike glare. "Tell me what I missed."

Alister shrugged and looked around at the crowded office. He put his hands in his pockets. "It's a long story," he said.

Professor Odd went over to a chair that had been tucked between two bookcases and dragged it over to the desk, where the woman—Raji—was busy typing away at a small computer. Carefully she sat down, and then picked up her feet and rested them on a corner of desk. (Raji glanced at the intruding shoes, looked like she was going to protest, then looked at Professor Odd's face and thought better of it.)

"So tell me your story, Mister Alister Bane," said Professor Odd. "I have *time.*"

THE GOOD MAN BANE

Part Two:

THE GOOD MAN BANE

ALISTER SAT IN THE DARK. His body ached, he felt dizzy and sick, and he wanted more than anything for the Professor to pry open his cell door and take him home.

This didn't happen, however, and as he sat in the dark, growing cold and stiff and beginning to see funny colors swooshing around in front of his eyes, he realized what a cruel irony it was. Because he was fairly certain that he *was* home, in a horrible, twisted way. He was back in the universe he'd started in, however long ago *that* was. (A year? Two years? Ten? Time was different in the Oddity, and Alister had taken to only counting the time he spent in actual universes, not floating in the void between.) But home . . . where was home, now? Was home his college dorm? But that had been stripped and bare the last time he'd seen it, and anyway it had never felt like much of a home—not properly.

Home to Alister had been a rambling stone house in the Old Country near Loch Galross, with hundred-year-old roses climbing over its crumbling front and a big, warm kitchen filled with his grandmother's cooking. Specifically his seventh and eighth summers, when he had the place to himself and was old enough to really start exploring and noticing things. Then they'd renovated it, put in modern plumbing and heating, and turned it into a Bed and Breakfast. It was still the same house, still the same stony exterior, and even the same roses growing up the outside, but it never quite felt like *home* after that. It was warmer and brighter, but it was always filled with new and strange people, and Alister had to be very careful whenever he left his room, otherwise he'd be pounced on and fawned over. It had been a relief, really, moving away for university, though Alister still missed the old town, with its little bookshop that had special-ordered his astronomy books so he didn't have to bus all the way to Stirling, the tea room with its ever-changing array of oddly flavored sweets, and the fishmonger who was old friends with his grandfather and would let Alister sweep the floor for chips.

The problem was *that* home didn't exist anymore. The old fishmonger had retired, and though his son had expanded the business, it no longer had the same, welcoming feel. The book-shop had been forced to close—there had been a coffee house chain opening in its place the last time Alister had been for a visit, which the tea room had been eyeing nervously. The old house was still there, but *that* hadn't felt like home since the renovation.

Alister was a little surprised to realize, as he curled up in the dark and resigned himself to a long wait, that the home he was pining after was a tear-drop shaped room lit by dim, colored lights, where the windows with pink, lacy curtains looked out into the void between universes, and a huge table covered in amazing and interesting things sat in the middle. A place where he had to climb a ladder to get up to his room, but it was large and comfortable, and he got to pick out a new, colorful shirt each time he woke up.

Home was Elo cooking a giant pan of scrambled ostrich eggs in the kitchen alcove, or sitting around the table drinking a hot, chocolatey beverage that came from an isolated monastery on Niatano, or watching movies displayed across all the Oddity's screens.

Home was a safe, cozy, crowded place where he could retreat to after days on sunny beaches, or at the tops of mountains, or touring castles, or—occasionally—having hair-raising adventures.

He could imagine that home so clearly that after a time Alister began *seeing* the Oddity's lights shifting into view before his eyes, and he realized he was seeing things in the dark again, so he shut them.

His cell contained a thin blanket and a hard pillow, and a bucket which needed no explanation. After a while Alister wrapped the blanket around his shoulders, curled up on the pillow, and in his perpetual waiting, eventually fell asleep.

He was woken some time later by his bladder, so he made careful use of the bucket before lying back down at the opposite end of the cell.

The next time he was woken it was because his cell door had opened, and someone was shining a light directly into his face. He raised a hand to shield himself, but a moment later someone stuffed a hood over his head, and then he was marched out of his cell.

Even in his frightened, half-awake state, he knew that the wrong people had come for him.

* * *

Interview Room 7 at Canary West was a small, cold, window-less room with sound-proofed walls. Agent Parthenon liked it because it felt secure and she knew where all the cameras were. It had a table and two chairs and a lot of hidden microphones, but she could access all their feeds and that was the important thing.

Currently it also had herself, seated in the chair facing the only door, and Specimen 1017, who was handcuffed to the chair opposite her. Parthenon thought the handcuffs were not strictly necessary considering how bewildered and disoriented the man was, but better safe than sorry. Parthenon was conscious of the privilege she had in conducting the initial interview, and she wasn't going to let anything ruin her day. Not even the Professor—Logistics had made sure of that.

Agent Parthenon narrowed her eyes at the man across from her, who blinked back out of red-rimmed, watery ones. (The only light in the room was angled so that it shone over her shoulder—not directly in the interviewee's face, just so that it made it painful for them to look at her.)

He was a young man, tallish and lanky, with short brown hair, strong dark eyebrows, and stubble over his chin. He could be considered handsome, Parthenon noted with profes-sional disinterest, if he didn't look so much like a lost, half-drowned rat. He was wearing the same shiny blue jacket—now a little singed and stained—and bright yellow-and-white paisley button-down shirt as he had been when they collected him, and this Parthenon noted in her log.

Pulling up the specimen's file, she frowned at the name it showed at the top.

"Alister . . . Galross . . . *Bane*," she said, leaving imposing gaps between the words. "Strange surname, for an Albian. You're not a crossborder brat, are you?"

The specimen's face twisted in annoyance. "That's my mother's name," he snapped. "*Her* name was Bain—with an I N instead of an N E. Changed it because there was another actress in Glascal named *E Bain*."

He certainly had the accent of an Albian, Parthenon noted. But not a Glascallian. His accent spoke of the southern highlands, but she wasn't enough of an expert to place him exactly.

"Yes, Evelyn Bane," said she said, making sure to sound as bored as possible. "Died of a heroine overdose at twenty-four. Disowned by her parents, her only child was then adopted by the father's parents, and raised in . . . Lochgalrosshead?"

Specimen 1017 sighed and slumped back in his chair. "My father's hometown. Grandmam said I got Galross as my middle name because Mum didn't care for *his* name."

"MacUpsaig," said Agent Parthenon, reading from the file. "Yes, I can agree with her there. And you were raised exclusively in Lochgalrosshead?"

"Sounds like you have my family genealogy all laid out in that nice file of yours," said the specimen. "It should be able to tell you *that* at least."

"No summer camping trips? No . . . inexplicable adventures as a child? You may only remember them as innocent, fun playtimes."

Specimen 1017 looked at her mulishly from under one cocked eyebrow. He had good, strong eyebrows, perfect for cocking, and had the ability to raise one independently of the other—something Parthenon had yet to master, to her ever-increasing frustration.

"I nearly drowned in Loch Galross when I was eight," he said, his tone arch and sarcastic. "Do you count near-death experiences as innocent, fun playtimes?"

In truth Agent Parthenon did, but only if they were *other people's* near-death experiences, and only if they were *near*-death ones, not *actual*-death ones. She made a note in the specimen's file though, mostly because she thought the action would annoy him.

"Our census shows your peers chose to pursue university in Alba," she said, changing the subject in the hopes of getting the man to admit something that way. "What brought you so far south?"

Specimen 1017 rolled his head back until it hung off the end of his chair, and stared at the ceiling. She saw his throat work as he swallowed, and his eyebrows knotted. Eventually he said:

"Weather seemed nicer," and shut his mouth firmly.

Agent Parthenon set down the file and her log and folded her hands over them to give 1017 a direct stare.

"You know, Mr. Bane, I cannot help you if you do not help *me.* Now, we know—"

She was cut off, however, by Specimen 1017 raising his head and beginning to shout at her.

"Help me?" he said, a little hoarse. "*Help* me? After you *kidnapped* me—twice!—and stuck me in a dark room overnight, and handcuffed me to a chair? You could give me a *drink,* or maybe some *breakfast*, or even, I don't know, *let me go home!* That'd help a lot, I tell you, and you don't need to know my childhood history or the reasoning behind my choice in university to do any of that!"

Agent Parthenon sighed. It was not an ideal response, but she'd managed to get a little material to work with. Enough that, she was reasonably certain, Dr. Carver would keep her on the case. She certainly hoped so. Specimen 1017 was a harder nut than he looked, and she was curious to find out what would make him crack.

Pressing a hidden button on her wrist, she said: "Terminate interview in seven, please," and then sat back and watched as two custodians came in and dragged the specimen—still shouting—away.

They put Alister, none too gently, back in the same cell as before. Unless it was another, identical one. The bucket was empty, anyway, and the place smelled of disinfectant. He'd knocked his elbow on something hard between there and that horrible room where he'd been interviewed, and for a while afterward he had to sit curled in a corner, nursing it and trying not to cry.

If he started to cry, Alister knew, he'd lose any control he had left over himself, and would probably go insane.

It had been a mistake to shout at that agent. But she had looked so smug, so satisfied, and so . . . well, like she wasn't seeing him as a real *person* at all. It had made him scared and angry, and he'd lost his temper.

What had brought him south, indeed! Like he was going to tell her all about the stupid row he'd had with Granddad over not taking a job straight out of school and "wasting his summer" building a telescope in the attic and how Grandmam had found him in tears in his room and said that she'd sent his marksheet to Baybridge, which had an excellent astronomy course in Gill College, and only asked that he come back afterward and make the whole of Lochgalrosshead proud.

Then again, maybe he should have, much as it shamed him. Losing his temper had probably killed any chance of getting food or—more importantly—water.

Were they just going to let him wither away and die in here? Well, they'd certainly never know his story if they did that! Unless they were just waiting for him to die in order to dissect him. Then Alister remembered how, when they'd found Dave, he'd been missing the tips of his arms, and shuddered.

The Canary Company didn't wait for you to die before it started cutting into you.

He was jerked out of his downward mental spiral by the scrape of metal as a small hatch at the bottom of the door to his cell was slid open.

Hope flared in his chest for an instant, only to be put out again when he saw it was not the Professor. It was a tray containing two plastic boxes, a foil-wrapped package, and a tiny water bottle. It looked like the kind of dinner tray one might get on an airplane, except there were no eating utensils.

Then the hatch was pulled shut, and Alister had to grope his way over and feel around until he found the tray again.

He drank the water in one go, then cautiously opened the containers and ate their contents using his fingers. This turned out to be a salad with some fruit, a piece of dry chicken, and a small, hard, baked potato.

Eating the potato was a mistake. It dried out Alister's mouth all over again and nearly stuck in his throat. He was thirstier than ever, but at least his stomach didn't hurt as much, and he didn't feel as dangerously dizzy. He pushed himself back up against the far wall and tried to think, but all his mind would do was spin worse and worse scenarios of what would happen if he wasn't rescued, and he fell to hoping so hard that ever nerve felt on fire and he jumped at the slightest sound, the faintest hint, of a door opening to another place altogether.

Agent Parthenon stood in the director's outer office—which was as close as anyone got to Dr. Carver these days—and looked directly at the dark little eye over the display screen showing a grainy depiction of his face. It was, she knew, the camera that fed what he saw on his own screen, and she'd noticed how much better the man responded when the image of *her* face seemed to be looking directly at him. As opposed to what he himself was doing: his camera was up and a little to the side of his screen, so what she saw was an indirect view of the side of his face. It made gauging his expressions difficult, but not impossible. Agent Parthenon fancied she was good with expressions, and right now, unless she was very much mistaken, Dr. Carver was torn between excitement, satisfaction, and fear.

The fear was evident in the twitch of his eyes, though not in the cadence of his voice, which was as rich and relaxed as ever as it came rolling out of the speaker in confident waves.

"Has he given any information about the manner in which he and Specimen 1016 have been jumping universes?"

"No, sir," said Agent Parthenon. "But I expect it was by the same machine that I encountered."

"Yes . . . and, previously—has he given you any clue as to his earlier travels?"

"No," said Agent Parthenon, not liking to give two negative answers in a row, but truthfulness was the better option here. Dr. Carver wasn't the best at spotting lies, but he always found out eventually, and when he did you were lucky if you were only fired. The Canary Company had an extremely strict non-disclosure agreement, and the more sensitive information you were exposed to, the worse you had it if there came a reckoning. So she sighed and went on.

"No, he hasn't admitted to anything directly. But he has corroborated our own research pertaining to his childhood. I've started a search for his father, but would you like me to bring his grandparents in, now?"

On the screen, Dr. Carver stroked his chin with a long, brown finger, and eventually shook his head. "Not yet," he said. "But keep them under observation. I want to see if he tries to contact them by . . . unusual methods."

"We stripped him of all his tech," Parthenon pointed out. "Not that he had much to be going on."

"Like I said," said Dr. Carver, tapping the tips of his fingers together, in the way he did when he was pleased with himself but didn't like to show it. "*Unusual* methods."

"Will do, sir," said Agent Parthenon. "Anything else?"

Dr. Carver thought about this for a little while, then said: "If he continues to be uncooperative, you have permission to take more direct measures. Oh, and see that he's properly scanned and catalogued."

Agent Parthenon saluted, and held it until her screen had gone dark—signifying the end of the interview. Turning on her heel she marched past the director's secretary—a thin, pale-faced man that put Parthenon in mind of a fish—and exited the outer office. As soon as she was in the hall she pulled out her in-house phone and hit the button for operator.

"Get me accounting," she said when prompted. Then, when a bored voice announced this was what she had, she went on: "Got a specimen for you. A re-log. Number 1017. Yes, *that* one. Custodians will be on hand—he's a live one." She hung up and, pocketing her phone, walked down the hall with a spring in her booted step, whistling softly.

After a while Alister fancied he could see shapes in the colors that swirled before his eyes from the lack of all other stimuli. They put him in mind of large-finned, slow-moving fish, and one looked so real—so solid and detailed—that he tried to put his hand out and touch it.

Of course his hand met empty air, but that didn't disturb the vision, which hung before his eyes until he closed them.

"Just *don't* start talking to them," he muttered to himself, letting his head rock back against the metal wall. Talking to *himself,* he reasoned, was perfectly fine, as long as it really was *himself* he was talking to.

"You'll get through this, Alister," he told himself, firmly. "The Professor's having a wee bit of trouble with one thing or another. Maybe there was temporal slippage or something, but she'll be here. She'll come."

In truth the idea of temporal slippage frightened Alister. It could mean he was in for a long wait if it slipped the wrong direction. It was more comforting to imagine that Professor Odd was already in this world, and just having a hard time getting to him—the Canary Company seemed to know enough about how the Oddity worked to be careful of the portal anchors it left available.

The problem with that was Alister kept half-expecting the Professor—or maybe Elo or even Dave—to open his cell door and set him free. So it was especially disappointing when the door opened—Alister had the presence of mind to shield his eyes this time—and a pair of masked people in hazmat suits reached in and dragged him out.

They were not exactly rough, but they weren't gentle either. They handled Alister as though he were an animal, like a dog, and spoke to him only in short, simple words. Like he was a dog.

Alister managed to keep himself together until they led him into a clean, white, sterile-looking room with metal rings bolted to the walls and a drain in the center. Then the delicate net that had been thrown over his instinctual urges to fight and run was shredded, and he kicked and flailed and got one of the suited figures a solid hit in the midsection, but the other one clapped a plastic cup over his mouth and nose, and between one panicked breath and the next Alister's mind went fuzzy and vague. It felt like he was swimming in his own mind, caught in waves of a milky liquid that surged up and washed out his vision.

They were stripping him, spraying him with something warm and wet, then toweling him off and putting him in plain, canvas trousers and a pullover shirt. They sat him on a stool, and one of them held his head steady while the other one mechanically shaved off his hair with a pair of clippers. Alister was aware of the sensation like the distant brush of a prickly wind, but overall he was too focused on staying conscious, on remembering where and who he was, to pay much attention to what was actually happening.

His mind kept slipping sideways, remembering how the Professor had described the experience of being lobotomized: as if her brain had gone like a smashed kaleidoscope, and at the suggestion, Alister's mind helpfully summoned up images of broken color and light, which filled his milky vision and threatened to drown him.

A flash of light. A small red eye was staring at him, then it was removed, and he looked down to see his hands were covered in ink, and they were pressing his fingers to a strip of white paper.

That was wrong. He wasn't a criminal. He shouldn't be here.

He struggled. Someone said, "Specimen is responding."

"So give him another hit," someone else said.

Something was placed over Alister's mouth again, and the smell of sticky sweetness flooded his nostrils, and then he was sinking, dragged down under the rising tide of milky, broken colors.

Darkness fell. It was so complete it took Alister a moment to realize he was awake. He blinked against the scratchy surface his face was resting on, confused. He didn't remember going to bed. He didn't remember his room being this dark.

Then he realized he wasn't *in* his bed *or* his room. He wasn't even in the Oddity, and with that the crushing despair came back.

He was lying on his side on the cold, hard floor of his cell, one arm up to provide a cushion for his head, his higher leg crooked at the knee to prevent him accidentally rolling onto his face.

Coming fully awake now, with a slight, lingering nausea in his throat, he realized his head was freezing, and the arm that had been doubling as a pillow was completely numb.

With a groan he rolled onto his back, using his good arm to bring the numb limb down and across his chest, massaging it gingerly through the pins and needles. He could feel the floor against the back of his head, and when he explored that area he found his hair had been reduced to a short stubble. The clothes he was wearing were coarse against his skin; they felt too large, and seemed to be made of canvas. They had even taken his shoes; his feet were freezing.

He was beginning to shake. Whether from withdrawal from drug they'd put in him, or from the growing lump of panic in his chest, he wasn't sure. Once he regained feeling in his arm he pushed himself into a sitting position and curled into the nearest corner, bringing his knees up into his chest and wrapping his arms around them.

The darkness pressed in on all sides, like a physical force, and it was with a twisted sense of relief that Alister saw the fuzzy, indistinct shapes of colorful fish begin to emerge before his eyes. At least that was *something.*

"Mister Bane," said a female voice unnervingly close to his ear.

It was both like and unlike the Professor's, and Alister had spent so long hoping that for a split second he thought it *was* her. But a part of him recoiled, knowing the speaker was someone very different, and so he only grunted in response. Inside, however, he felt like a glass plate had broken under the momentary relief. He was all sharp edges, and it hurt.

He was glad it was dark; at least they couldn't see him cry.

"Mister *Bane,*" said the voice, and this time he recognized it as belonging to the bronze-skinned woman who had interviewed him earlier.

"*What?*" snapped Alister, stifling a sniff.

"This could have gone much more pleasantly for you, if you had been honest with us from the beginning."

The voice sounded as though it was coming from somewhere up and to the right. A hidden speaker, Alister guessed.

"What do you *think* I've been doing?" he asked, spitting the words out.

"There's no need to take that tone," said the voice, reproachfully. "You know as well as I do how important our work is."

"No, I *really* don't," said Alister.

"Every precaution must be taken in the face of an infinity of threats," said the voice, as if quoting something. "*You,* well. We're not sure if you're a threat or not. Since you have behaved uncooperatively from the start, we must assume you are a threat. If you have information that implies otherwise, you can help yourself by sharing it with us."

"*Me,* a threat?" Alister said, stifling a hoarse laugh. If he started laughing, he knew, it would quickly turn to screams, and then he wouldn't be able to stop. And then, because he figured whatever he said could not possibly make his situation any worse, he went on: "I'm *no one.* I'm just a bloke from a nowhere town in Alba. I'm a . . . *was* a university student. I'm no one special. I had a completely ordinary and boring life until *you* lot came along and *erased* me. And since then I've done nothing—*nothing*—to harm this world! I haven't even been *in* this world!"

"Nothing?" said the voice icily. "Then it was *not* you who deactivated our operations on Canary 6?"

Alister swallowed. There had been the time he and the Professor had intercepted a party of genetically modified dogs who were attempting to ship research and tech to the Canary Company through a naturally occurring wormhole. It had certainly seemed like the better option for the dogs, whose society had been held back by the Company's interference.

"You'd no right to be messing about with them," he said instead.

"And you continue to refuse to share the technology by which you facilitated your prior travels," the voice went on, as if it had not heard.

"*What* prior travels?" moaned Alister. "I never went—" he broke off with a gulp.

He *had* gone off world before the Canary Company had first captured him. For barely half an hour, he'd been given tea in the Oddity, and then returned to his class moments after he'd left. And when the Company had scanned him, something had come up on their radar. Which was why they'd kept him, erased all evidence of his life and treated him like an object.

"Look," he said, taking a deep, steadying breath. "Something you've *got* to understand. I only ever *visited* the Oddity before you got me. And it was by *accident*. I *promise* you I'm nothing special."

Silence. It lasted so long Alister thought the voice had gone away, and was just beginning to see the colorful fish again, when it cut through his half-dreaming with a sound like a snarl.

"Your prevarication is telling," it hissed, sending a chill down Alister's spine. "The Dustings test doesn't lie. You *are* holding something back, and until you comply, your situation will continue to become more uncomfortable, Mister Bane."

Alister shut his eyes and leaned his head back against the wall with a soft thump.

"*More uncomfortable*," repeated the voice. There was a faint click, and then nothing.

Uncomfortable turned out to be an understatement. Things went downright *unbearable* after that conversation, though it was such a slow build Alister didn't realize how bad things were at once.

The first thing that happened was they pulled him out of his cell, stuffed a bag over his head, and marched him to another cell which, once the bag came off, was pitch black. Feeling around, Alister found the expected bucket, which seemed to be bolted to the floor, and a small pile of bedding. The ceiling was lower— he couldn't stand up completely straight—and there were no windows at all, just a small ventilation duct with a heavy grill over it, securely bolted down.

Food no longer came in plates, but in thick, plastic bowls. It was the consistency of cold porridge, but tasted slightly meaty.

Out of curiosity more than anything else, Alister left his bowl on the far side of his cell one time, to see if someone would come in to get it. He hadn't seen a living person since the people in hazmat suits, and he hadn't seen a human face since the interview with the company agent. A part of him wanted to make sure that *people* still existed—even though he knew they must: the bucket periodically retracted through a hole in the wall and came back empty.

No one came, but instead the little flap cracked open, and something that scratched on the hard floor was poked inside. Curious, Alister felt for it, and just had time to close his fingers around the long, thin wire, when an electric shock burned his hands, and he let go with a yelp.

He heard muffled laughter from beyond the door, and someone said, "That'll learn ya," and then the wire found the bowl, hooked it, and dragged it out.

Alister left his bowls right next to the door after that. If the people outside were anything like the owner of the voice he'd heard, they could go disappear for all he cared.

Time stretched. Not in the tranquil, ageless way it stretched in the Oddity. This was the agonizing pull of monotony that went on forever and ever, spreading Alister's mind thin across it.

The colorful fish came and went. Sometimes he heard voices, and though at first he was careful to make a distinction between real noises and the voices in his head, when the latter turned out to be the *only* voices he heard, eventually he took to listening to what they said out of sheer boredom.

"Have you tried *talking* to them?" Professor Odd asked him. Alister could see her crouched, her pose a mirror of his own, against the opposite wall. And because he could see her, he knew this was all in his imagination. It was his brain trying to fill in the empty gaps by pure invention.

Well, maybe he could help himself help himself, as it were.

"Yes, I've *tried* that," he told the apparition. "They won't *listen.*"

"Not the agent," said the ghost of Professor Odd, with a shake of her head. She wasn't wearing a wig, and the green leopard spots that dotted her skull stood out luridly against the pale skin, while her tentacle curled lazily over one shoulder. It twitched as she went on: "The people in suits. The ones giving you *food.* Everyone here who actually knows what's going on will be too invested in what they're doing to admit that it's wrong. Try talking to the grunts. The custodians. The people who are feeding you. *They're* the ones who might actually listen. Listening to orders is what got them into their position in the first place; who says they won't listen to you?"

It was a mad idea. And as it came from Alister's own brain, he wondered if this meant he was also going mad.

But he was desperate. After who-knew how long in the cool, dark, lonely cell which was beginning to smell, with barely enough to eat and drink, dried not-porridge caked on his hands and his back cramping from not being able to straighten all the way, he was willing to try anything.

The next time he was fed, Alister took the empty bowl and put it in the corner farthest from the slot, and when the wire came, tapping and probing, he leant down by the opening and said:

"If you want the bowl back, just say *please.*"

The tapping of the wire paused, and then a man's voice, very close on the other side of the door, said: "Don't get cocky, son, or I'll open this door and take your brain apart myself, no matter what Parthenon says."

It was a overpowering sensation, hearing another human's voice again, and having it be so unfriendly. It made Alister's head pound, and he went and crouched beside his bucket while the wire fished his food bowl out and the flap slid shut.

He didn't have the heart to try again right away. But he started paying attention to the *manner* in which the food bowl was placed in his cell. He noticed how, on some occasions, there was a sharp *smack* of the dish hitting the floor; half the time the slop inside spilled. Other times it was slipped inside with more care. Almost *considerately.* When Alister moved his bowl out of reach after it had been placed in his cell, rather than tossed, it seemed the person behind the wire was a little less sure of themselves, and it took longer for them to find the bowl.

After the shock of the first voice had worn off, Alister tried again—this time after the considerate person had fed him.

He took his bowl and knelt at the far end of the cell. He waited. There was a whisper of metal as the slot slid open, and when he heard the tap of the wire he said:

"I can give you the bowl back, if you'd only *ask*."

There was a gasp from the other side of the door, and a clatter that sounded like whoever was behind the wire had dropped it.

"Hello?" said Alister, his chest so full of hoping that he could barely speak.

The wire resumed its tapping, but more shakily, now.

"Just *ask*," said Alister. "I'll put it down right by the slot, no tricks."

The tapping stopped. Very faintly, as though it was coming through a layer of steel and concrete by way of a narrow tube, a female, South-London voice said:

"Sorry. They didn't say you could speak . . . "

A joyful chorus rose up inside Alister's mind. Professor Odd gave him the thumbs-up from her corner of his cell, and he had to blink hard to dispel the hallucination so he could continue.

"Why shouldn't I?"

"Just didn't expect it, is all." The owner of the voice—which was light and pleasant and sounded like music to Alister's starved ears—coughed. "Er, *could* I have the bowl back?"

Alister didn't want to give the bowl back. Giving the bowl back would mean the speaker would go away, and he'd be alone with his overactive imagination again. But a part of him reasoned that this same person had been feeding him regularly, and would likely feed him again. And he *had* said . . .

Reluctantly he crept forward and slipped the bowl into the slot, wincing away when he felt his fingers brush the wire—but it didn't shock him this time.

The bowl retreated, followed by the wire, but the slot didn't close. After a while, the voice said:

"Thank you."

"You're welcome," said Alister, miserably.

"Er . . . " said the voice, and Alister held his breath. "Why do you sound Albian?"

"Because that's where I'm *from*," Alister replied.

"Oh," said the voice. Then: "I'm probably not meant to know that."

"Probably not," said Alister.

"Right, I should . . . er . . . be going."

"Come back," Alister called into the slot, before it could close. "I'll tell you more things you're not meant to know!"

But he said it to the closed slot; the person on the other side probably hadn't heard.

Still, it was good to have spoken to someone outside his own head. Alister went and curled up in his favorite corner, hugging the memory to himself.

"It's not much," said Elo, who had taken the Professor's place. "But it's a start."

Alister agreed.

The friendly feeder did not come back after Alister had spoken to her. It was all messily delivered food and angry, stabbing wires when Alister tried to hide his bowl.

"Don't worry," said Elo, when Alister was curled tightly in on himself, crying so hard he could barely breathe. "It'll get better soon, I promise."

She gave him one of her earnest, canine smiles, and Alister wished, with every fiber of his being, that she was real. How he wanted to wrap himself around that strong, soft, furry body, and feel the warm, wet gust of her breath. But when he crawled over to the corner it was cold and empty, and he had to scream for a while after that. He only stopped when his throat got so sore it hurt too much.

Someone must have heard him, though, because the door opened and another pair of masked, besuited people reached in for him.

It as worse this time. Monumentally worse. They did not drug him: they held him down while they clipped the short fuzz that had grown over his head and face, and then pushed him under a heavy spray of water that started too cold and ended too hot. They blasted him with hot air instead of toweling him dry, which left his skin parched and papery, and finally they stuffed him into another pair of simple, canvas trousers and pullover shirt. These were a tannish color, Alister noticed, and had PROPERTY OF THE CANARY COMPANY stenciled in black on the back of the shirt. He wondered, dully, if that referred to the clothes or to him.

At the end they sat him down in a chair, in a room that was both too bright and too dark at the same time. It had been so long, and Alister's brain had spent so long spinning out in the dark and silence of his cell, that it wasn't until the bronze-skinned woman with the long, aquiline nose and sharp, black hair walked inside that he realized he was back in the interview room. *An* interview room, anyway. It looked just like the last one, but for all he knew they had dozens, just the same.

The woman—whose name tag said Parthenon in neat, black letters—put a manilla folder on the table and began carefully arranging the papers in it so they were laid out in front of her. Alister tried reading them upside-down, but could only make sense of the headers ("Education" and "Previous Travels" jumped out at him).

Mostly, however, he felt numb and cold and a little itchy. After so long in the dark the light hurt his eyes, making them water. He found himself blinking up at Parthenon, humiliated and miserable.

"Mister *Bane,*" she said, in a voice calculated to rake on nerves already made raw by his rough treatment and sensory deprivation. "Now that you understand what uncooperative behavior entails, I am hopeful you will be slightly more . . . *obliging.*"

Alister wanted to upend the table and shove it into Parthenon's smug, pointed face, but they'd shackled him to his chair, and besides, he didn't think he had the strength. Something inside him crumpled, and he leaned back with a groan. He found himself staring at the ceiling of the room: it was metal with peeling, white paint. Alister thought he could make out landscapes in the sharp, angular cracks—mesas and buttes, with canyons and valleys between.

He blinked, trying to get his brain to anchor in reality, but it kept sliding off sideways.

"What do you want to know?" he asked, his voice sounding fuzzy and indistinct even to himself

"We just want to know about your previous travels, Mister Bane," said Parthenon, with the sort of sweetness that put Alister in mind of cold medicine.

"There've been rather a lot," mumbled Alister. "There was Niatano . . . and the bubble world . . . and the dragon world . . . and the one inside the machine . . . the Professor gets around, you know?"

"Yes," said Parthenon, her voice icy and brittle. "I know. But I was asking about your *previous* travels. *Before* you met the Professor."

With a great effort Alister raised his head to stare at the woman. He knew he couldn't read expressions the same way Professor Odd could, but she looked perfectly sincere to him.

"*What* travels?" he asked. "My summer trips to Glenfinnan?"

"No," said Parthenon. "I mean your previous travels to worlds other than this one."

"I didn't *have* any travels to worlds other than this one," Alister wailed. "Not before I met the Professor!"

"Then why did you register as a partially alien entity when you were first scanned?" asked Parthenon, her words pointed. They stabbed at Alister's soft, mushy brain like needles, making him wince.

"I don't *know*," said Alister, letting his head fall back to stare at the ceiling again. The landscape had changed while he was away: now it looked like the world with the lightning canyon, where he'd found the man chained to the rock. There was even a sharp zigzag of broken paint, where the metal showed through, reminding him both of the impossible stone formation, and the cracks of void that showed through later.

He jerked himself. He'd been asked a question. He needed to respond.

"Maybe it was because I'd already *been* out of this universe when your lot picked me up—*with* the Professor," he said, trying not to sound sarcastic. Getting Parthenon to believe him was his best chance at getting out of this with his wits, let alone his life. But it was as though his brain could no longer fully control his mouth, and the words flowed out like acid over his tongue.

"That's all there is: I was as monoversal as all of you! Then I meet her and *bam!* Hiya, this car door leads to a place between worlds! Heya, your universe isn't the only one. Oh, also the dog can talk and your substitute tutor is a strange alien lady with a tentacle growing out the back of her head! *That's all there is!*"

He looked back down, only to find Parthenon staring at him grimly.

"No," she said, quietly. "No that's *not*, Mr. Bane. We have incontrovertible evidence that you made extensive, unauthorized trips to other universes before you were abducted and brainwashed by the Professor—"

"I wasn't—!" Alister began, weakly, but Parthenon's words rolled over him like a tractor.

"—which was *also* a breach of our laws—"

"Who says *you* get to make—"

"—and leaves us with no recourse but to treat you as a Level 6 Priority Subject. Now, you can cooperate, and you will be given as much autonomy as we feel it is safe to allow—"

"I *am* cooperating!" Alister ground out.

"—but if you continue to hinder our work, you will be archived."

That didn't sound good at all, but Alister was so angry, frightened, and off balance by this point that he didn't care.

"What do you not understand about 'I did not go traveling to other universes before I met the Professor?'" he snapped, seeing spittle fly from his own lips. "What do you not understand about *I'm telling you the truth already?* Is it too much to admit that you were *wrong*?"

Parthenon's mouth pinched in at this, and she whispered something into her collar. A moment later two suited men stepped into the room and approached Alister.

At this point Alister's brain gave up its tenuous hold on rationality, and he began to kick and scream inarticulately. Adrenaline filled his veins. He didn't even feel the needle going in, and only knew he had been drugged in a distant way, as his vision clouded over and everything went black.

This time Alister dreamed. As the drugs loosed their hold on his brain he dreamed of cracked landscapes that fell apart under his fingers. He dreamed a new childhood for himself, in which the attic door in the old house outside Lochgalrosshead really did lead to another world. It was a world just like his, only everything that was normally silver glimmered with all the colors of the rainbow. The next time he went through the door, he was on an alien planet with a purple sky and tall, mint-colored plants like giant dandelions—puffy, spherical blossoms on long, thin stalks that reached up far above his head. He found one flower that had fallen down, and he was able to see that it was over three feet across, and the little flowers were actually the crinkled wings of moths. Moths made of petals, though. He later learned that they were not moths, but an alien species that grew from the flower at the top of the stalk. When they were fully developed they spread their wings, causing the flower to bloom, before flying off to fertilize other flowers, thus repeating the cycle.

Why had he never told Professor Odd about these memories? She would have loved to hear about the strange flower-insects. She might already know of them, and they could go back to that world. Alister dearly missed that world—it had smelled sweet, like honey and ice cream, and the ground had been soft and squishy.

It was only as he drifted closer to consciousness, becoming aware of the hard, cold metal under his cheek, the cramp in his elbow, and the faint smell of disinfectant, that he remembered that it was a *dream*, not a memory. Parthenon was *wrong,* no matter how much she seemed to be convinced otherwise.

Yes, said someone inside Alister's head. *You can still distinguish fact from fantasy. Things could be worse.*

Now he was hallucinating Dave, Alister thought, miserably. He didn't want to go from one dream to another. He wanted reality, but reality was so horrible he couldn't bear to face it.

I am sympathetic to your predicament. I was once put in a similar position. I survived, and so will you, said Dave—not in his harsh, abrasive, synthetic voice, but in the smooth, cool tones that Alister remembered permeating his mind when Dave spoke to him directly, through his slime. Alister felt something wet run down his cheek, and cursed himself for crying so easily. He was missing Dave—*Dave* of all people!—he must be in a very bad state.

You are in a suboptimal mental state, it is true, said Dave. *But it is less disintegrated than I had feared. I am also touched that you missed me, but mostly I am sorry. It took far longer than I had anticipated.*

Alister wondered what Dave could be talking about. What took longer than anticipated?

Getting here, said Dave. *But, as you humans say, better late than never, correct?*

Alister squeezed his eyes shut. If only Dave *was* here.

But, said Dave. *I am.*

It was only then that Alister came fully awake. He realized that his head was strangely warm at about the same time he realized the wet things running down his cheeks were not tears but drops of slime. Then his brain registered the smooth slide of little feelers wriggling across his scalp, dipping into his ears; he could not open his right eye because there was an arm with gently grasping suckers draped over it. More arms twined around his head, running down his neck (but not around it) to lie across his shoulders.

He shot up abruptly, pulling his knees up and crawling backward until he hit the wall.

Careful, warned Dave, and Alister felt his muscles go limp as the consistency of the slime changed subtly. *I am highly squishable like this, and it won't help anyone if I am injured!*

Still disbelieving, Alister raised a hand and slowly wiped the slime from his left eye. He felt the side of one of Dave's arms—

comparatively cool and smooth and slick with slime—and rather than pull away, he let his hand linger.

Could you hallucinate a solid object? he wondered.

Quite possibly, said Dave. *Never underestimate the capacity of the human brain to delude itself. As it happens, however, I am not an hallucination: I am real and present in this narrative, as are you, and as such we are both in grave danger. I need you to listen to me, Alister Bane, but most of all, I need you to trust me. Can you do that?*

The wetness on Alister's face *was* from tears now, but this time he felt no shame. No matter whether Dave was really here, or if he was simply an extension of Alister's own brain, the answer was the same:

"Aye," said Alister, his voice a hoarse wreck. "Aye, I trust you."

Rajinder Ayoadé pushed the trolly laden with bowls down the narrow aisles of the high-security animal ward. The place had always given her the creeps, and now coming back after two months, it was even worse. The flat, metal doors with the food-flaps at the bottom, like mean little mouths, and the single peep-hole in the center—Rajinder hadn't dared look inside after what she had seen the first time; an animal that contorted should not be alive, she felt, and had been sick afterwards.

But the Canary Company paid their techs well, even if they were junior techs, and even if they hadn't got the best marks from university. The nondisclosure agreements were draconian, but they also didn't seem to care that her parents had come from the two regions on earth that were the most at odds with Greater

Britain, and even though she was literally a black sheep in a sea of whites, on the whole her coworkers were decent people, and the work itself was interesting: searching for evidence of other universes *sounded* crazy, until you saw some of the artifacts that the Company had found.

It was just the high-security animal ward that got her down, especially after the time one of them had spoken to her. A talking dog or large cat was something Rajinder was not quite ready to accept, even at this point. Not, she told herself, because she didn't think they could exist, but because a part of her knew that, if an animal could speak like a human, that meant it could think like a human, which meant it could probably *feel* like a human, which meant it had no business being locked up in such a horrible little cell.

And they were horrible cells. Rajinder had to clean them out when they were vacated, and even though she jammed the door open behind her, so there was no chance of her accidentally being shut in, she still felt like the place was pushing in on her, like it wanted to crush her. They were so small and narrow and isolating. A human would go crazy in there.

So she'd asked for a transfer, which had been granted, but now her replacement had got the flu, and she was the only Junior Tech with the training to make the hi-sec animal rounds. It had been with a clench of her stomach that she noticed Specimen 1017 was still in his same cell, and when it came time to push the little bowl through the slot, she did it with her fingertip, and then quickly moved on before she could hear anything from within. She finished her rounds without incident, cleaned out the two newly vacated cells, washed her hands, and had her own lunch.

She was almost in a cheerful mood by the time she made her second round, picking up the empty dishes. When she reached 1017's cell she hesitated, but when she put her hand in she felt the bowl right away, and no voice spoke.

She straightened up, holding the bowl, and something exploded in her mind.

There were words—there must have been words—but they were wrapped up in emotions and feelings and hard to make out. Mostly, she was struck by a sense of desperate loneliness, of fear and despair and a little bit of anger. It was so sudden, and so strong, that she staggered backwards, knocked into her trolly, and fell down.

Her hands were tingling where they held the bowl, so she dropped it, but the thoughts and feelings continued to assault her, and now the words came through strong enough that she could make sense of them.

Help. Help. You must help. They are hurting me. Let me out. Let me go. Help. Please, help.

The message repeated, over and over again, like a tape on loop. The longer Rajinder sat there, however, feeling her heart thudding in her chest, the stronger it got. After a while, it began to change. The rush of emotions diminished, replaced by a growing sensation of numbness and cold.

Open the door, Rajinder, said the words. It was not a voice. She heard nothing, but the meaning appeared in her head out of the swirl of confused feelings. These words had a different flavor than the cry for help, as though they came from a different person. A person who was not scared or lonely, but was, in a distant way, deeply angry.

"I can't," she whispered. "Don't know the code."

The release sequence is eight, eight, eight at first prompt, twenty-seven at second prompt, one, zero, one, seven at third prompt, the security word is technetium, *like your chemical element, and the colors are red, red, green, red, blue, purple. The activation word is* clear.

"I *can't . . .* " Rajinder whispered, but the words went on: they seemed to be a recording as well, and had answered her implied question by accident.

The release sequence can only be entered by a native human. Open the door, Rajinder. The release sequence is . . .

And the words went through her head again. And again. And *again.*

Eight, eight, eight at the first prompt. Twenty-seven at the second prompt.

"I *can't,*" she moaned.

One, zero, one, seven at the third prompt.

"Please," said a voice on the other side of the door. It was hoarse and weak, but it was still recognizable as the one that had spoken before.

The security word is technetium, *like your chemical element.*

"I don't know what you are!"

And the colors . . .

"My name is Alister Bane, I'm a human from this world, just like you."

. . . are red, red, green . . .

"Then why are you locked up?"

. . . red, blue . . .

"Someone made a mistake. Please, I promise I won't hurt you."

. . . purple.

"How do I know that?"

The activation word . . .

"I gave you the bowl back, didn't I?"

. . . is clear.

The spinning in Rajinder's head slowed, though the words continued to repeat. Now she was beginning to feel nauseated, a cold sweat breaking out all over her skin and her breath quickening.

"If I let you out will you stop talking inside my head?"

. . . like your chemical element.

"Yes."

Shakily, Rajinder got to her feet.   This was worse—inconceivably worse—than simply talking to a high security specimen. But she could always say later that she'd been mind-controlled. It wasn't even a complete lie.

She felt torn up inside: Specimen 1017 was probably a dangerous alien. There had to be a reason he was locked up. There *had* to be, because if Specimen 1017 was a human, then what the Company was doing to him was unforgivable. It would up-end everything Rajinder believed about the order of her life. She was one of the *good* guys.

Good guys didn't lock people up in dark cells and feed them dog food.

Good guys got people out of places like that.

Eight, eight, eight . . .

Rajinder pressed the key three times, and was prompted for a confirmation number.

Twenty-seven . . .

Then one, zero, one, seven. When the display switched to letters and asked for a security word she worried briefly that "technetium" might have been spelled with two l's, but her first guess must have been correct, because the panel switched to a color box, and she carefully tapped the screen on red, red, green, red, blue, and purple. A ding prompted the activation word, and in the steadiest voice she could muster, Rajinder said:

"Clear."

The heavy door let out a hiss as the lock disengaged, and Rajinder stepped back. The words were still repeating in her head, and she collapsed against the trolley, sliding to the floor and sitting there, trying not to be sick.

There was a whisper of movement on the other side of the door, and slowly it swung open—barely clearing Rajinder's feet—and someone came staggering out of the cell.

He was a man. A tallish man, skin so white it was almost translucent, with deep, sunken eyes and bony hands and wrists where they protruded from the end of his shapeless canvas shirt. He towered over her, yet leaned heavily on the doorframe, blinking against the light.

His head was covered by a bright green *thing* with countless tentacle-arms curling around his face and draping over his shoulders. Pale, greenish slime covered his skin, dripping from his nose and staining the neck of his shirt. Half his face was covered by a slimy green tentacle, and his one eye, when it found Rajinder, was red-rimmed and brown.

With a visible effort he unstuck his mouth and said: "'M sorry about this," and bent over her.

Rajinder cowered away, fearful of anything such a person might apologize for in advance. But the man only touched her lightly on the forehead, and the voice that had been on repeat in her mind abruptly vanished. The words *thank you* flashed briefly behind her eyes, and then all was quiet.

Save the groans of the man, who had stumbled into the hall and encountered the trolley, which slid sideways under his weight as he tried to steady himself. Rajinder grabbed it to keep from being run over, but couldn't muster the courage to help the man, much as she wished she could.

Instead she sat and stared as he staggered off down the hall. With his back to her, she could see that the tentacles converged on a round body the size of a pie pan, with a single, yellow-and-orange eye glaring at her from the center. She held the creature's gaze until the man dragged himself around the nearest corner, and the strange duo was lost to sight.

"I think 'm gonna be sick," Alister mumbled aloud, mostly out of habit.

Dave's arms tightened slightly around his shoulders.

You can make it.

"I *cannae* make it," Alister whined. His vision was blurry and the slime kept getting in his eye. He felt dizzy and weak, and feared that any moment men in hazmat suits would descend upon them. "We're in the middle of the *Canary Company*," he pointed out. "We can't just *walk out*."

No, we cannot. But you must continue to walk for now. Walk to the end of the hall, then turn right up the stairs.

Alister nearly broke down crying at the thought of stairs, but he somehow made it to the end of the hall, and there *were* stairs, with a railing he could clutch and heave himself along. He had to stop every third or fourth step and lean his head against the wall.

We are losing time, Dave told him, and Alister felt an arm slipping down the back of his shirt. It tickled a little, making him twitch. *Your escape has been noticed. You must climb.*

"What's the *point?*" Alister moaned. His saliva felt thick and he was having trouble catching his breath.

Freedom, said Dave. *But you must summit these stairs.*

"I *can't . . .* " gasped Alister.

I can, said Dave.

This confused Alister. In his confusion he raised his head, and at the same time heard voices shouting in the hall below them. He had to move.

He *couldn't* move. His atrophied muscles and weak body were being strained to the breaking point, and he felt like he was about to crack.

Trust me, said Dave, and though his voice was silent, spoken in thoughts and feelings and images, Alister thought his tone had taken on a hint of desperation.

"Y'can't mean . . . " he began.

I can if I must, said Dave. *It appears I must do so, for both our sakes. I have no wish to go back into that tank.*

Belatedly Alister realized that Dave had just as much to fear from the Canary Company as he did. Perhaps more. That made him feel terrible all over again, for forcing Dave into this situation.

But Dave had come. Dave had come *for him.* It seemed the least he could do was cooperate.

"Do what you have to," he wheezed. "I'll try to help."

Just continue to breathe, said Dave, and all his arms clamped down at once.

For Alister, his body went fuzzy and distant, as it did when he was falling asleep. Except now it was in violent motion, running jerkily up the steps. He felt his toe stub against the metal with numb detachment, saw the two suited figures waiting for them at the top and could do nothing to stop his charge or change his course.

His muscles tingled from whatever Dave was covering him in, and he ran, so fast he did forget to breathe, barreling into the figures and tearing past them.

They let him go, because all that lay beyond was a solid wall. Alister saw the scraped metal surface rushing at him, and closed his one eye in preparation for the impact . . .

. . . and fell softly into darkness, landing on something which gave under him, like a net. His mouth opened, and he had the surreal experience of hearing Dave use his own head as a slime-to-audio translator.

"We have pursuers!" Dave announced through Alister, somehow managing to sound synthetic and irritated, even when using a human voice.

"Shifting the portal 90 degrees," said a voice with a heavy Slavic accent.

There was an expectant silence, then the Slavic voice said: "Not pursued anymore, my ten-armed friend. I take you are our man Bane?"

"Yes," said Dave through Alister, and then receded, his arms loosening, and Alister felt the sensations from his body become more immediate. His toe smarted something terrible. He groaned.

"Cut it a wee bit close there, dint ya?" asked another voice. A voice with an unmistakable Edinburgh brogue, but a slight lisp that suggested some unconventional teeth.

Alister blinked his one available eye open, and found that this darkness was nowhere near as complete as that in his cell. It was only the dimness that came from having a few racks of red LEDs as a light source. They were more than enough to illuminate the crowd of people who were leaning over Alister, their whiskery faces twitching in interest.

He was surrounded by half a dozen large, bipedal rats, each wearing a slightly modified version of a silver jumpsuit with a wide, metal collar—as if there were helmets somewhere that sealed on over them—and each with a small metal box strapped to their necks. In size they were only as big as a large cat, but that was still far bigger than any rat Alister had seen. Their faces, though perfectly murine, held a similar level of intelligence and character as Elo's, and their expressions of interest, concern, and amusement (in one) were all eerily human.

I will leave you with the Rats of Alnitak, said Dave. *I require rest now.* He curled his arms under himself, leaving only two looped around Alister's shoulders, so he could cling to the back of his neck, and Alister felt his presence recede from the cold slime that still covered his head. And with it, much of Alister's own consciousness fell dormant as well.

Things took on a dreamlike quality after that, even though Alister knew this time it was no dream. He was aware of sights and sounds and physical sensations, but they had become detached from meaning.

He saw one of the rats—a smallish, brown one with a mangled right ear—come forward and extend a small, pink paw.

"Good to meet you, Alister Bane," a voice said in his ear, and even though he didn't see the animal's mouth move, he knew it was the rat which had spoken. "The Professor has told us much about you; it is an honor to meet you at last."

"He's got a chip," said the Slavic voice from earlier.

"No time," said the Edinburgh brogue. "We'll deal with that after we rendezvous with Retrieval Bound."

"And you'll let *me* do it," said another Slavic voice, deeper and angrier.

"Then let's get him in the sling and move out!"

Alister felt himself nudged and prodded gently, and he rolled along as best he could. He was wrapped up in a heavy cloth, then dragged laboriously onto a hard surface which rolled under his weight.

"I hope ye have a strong stomach, laddie," said the Edinburgh brogue, and a weight settled on his chest.

Alister tried to answer, but his mouth had gone thick and he couldn't get it open.

"He's shutting down," muttered the big, Slavic voice, and something sharp jabbed into Alister's arm. He groaned.

"That should keep you from crashing on us until we make rendezvous . . . "

"Everyone aboard?" someone called, and another answered, from around his feet:

"Good to go, Leader!"

Then there was a lurch and they began to roll.

What came next was almost worse, in a way, than everything that had come before. Alister was aware only of a mad plunge through darkness, of a smell like old sewage, and a few places where it felt like they went upside-down. A cool, damp wind scraped at his face, chilling the places still covered by Dave's slime.

Alister didn't know much. He didn't know the rats, or how they'd gotten here, or where they were taking him. But he also knew he was no longer in his cell, and that this wasn't a dream, and that was enough to keep him awake, keep him aware, and most of all keep him present.

Agent Parthenon sat in her office, the lights dimmed to the faintest glimmer, the screen of her monitor casting her face in harsh blue. The only sound was the faint click of her fingers skittering over the keys, and occasionally the whisper of outgoing breath.

The case of 1017 bothered her, like an itch she couldn't reach. She'd had stubborn subjects before—more stubborn than Alister Bane—and they had broken. They had revealed all. That was part of why she could wear the little, golden, dog-head pin of a Company Officer.

Alister Bane—*Specimen 1017,* Parthenon had to remind herself—was not that stubborn, really. True, she'd *thought* he was because he hadn't admitted to his extra-universal travels right away, but the more she had observed him the more she got the feeling he wasn't strong enough to lie for this long.

And that was wrong. The truth *couldn't* be what he was saying (correction: it *wasn't* what he was saying), and yet he seemed to think he *was* telling the truth.

Could the Professor have wiped his memory of his previous travels? Parthenon wouldn't have put it past her, though the thought didn't strike her as being quite right.

Nothing struck her as being "quite right," and that bothered her. It bothered her because Parthenon liked being quite right. She liked it enough that she could admit she was wrong and change her opinions in order to keep on being right, or so she liked to believe. But now all these conflicting facts were giving her a simmering feeling of unease. As though there were a bigger picture she was somehow missing, and no matter how far she pulled back from the situation, she still couldn't see it.

So she went over the data they had collected again and again, while she waited for her next chance to interview the man Bane.

Alister Bane was between 22 and 24 years of age, depending on how time had passed for him since he escaped from the Company. He had had some unknown level of extra-universal experience before being abducted and brainwashed by Professor Odd—Specimen 1016—and since then had traveled to at least one of the Company's subject worlds. He had been involved in the abortion of Loyal Dog, and had also likely been present—

along with the Professor—on universe F34. He left little birds made of folded paper as his calling card, and was thought to have the ability to pilot the Professor's strange ship.

Agent Parthenon shuddered at the memory of that place. It had been so alien, so incomprehensible, and she'd gotten the inexplicable feeling—which she hadn't felt since she was six and snuck into her grandmother's bedroom to go through the old woman's jewelry case—of being somewhere she wasn't supposed to be. It was almost an accident that what little data she had managed to collect had allowed Defense to generate a temporal block on spontaneous portals—but who knew how long that would last.

She'd had Alister—*Specimen 1017*—for almost six months. It was only a matter of time before the Professor came for him, she was certain. And while he was cracking, what she could glimpse of his insides didn't tally with what she'd been told to expect.

Somehow, that troubled her more than it should have.

Round and round she chased her feelings of discomfort, until she dug in her heels and put in a request to see the director. This was unusual, but Parthenon had spoken with Dr. Carver more than any other operative since she'd brought Specimen 1017 home, and she felt it was likely her request would be granted. She was in the middle of sending the forms when her comm went off in alarm.

Parthenon jumped at the sudden sound, then spun around in her chair as she recognized the tone: it was a breach alarm. Someone, somewhere, had gotten out of containment—and in her paranoid mindset she knew exactly who it was.

She paged Caruthers and Villafranka, then dispatched a unit of custodians to the hi-sec animal ward, all while in the process of putting on her encounter gear.

If Bane was out, it meant he'd had help. Which meant the Professor. Agent Parthenon could feel the blood pounding in her ears, her heart racing at the thought of meeting Specimen 1016 again, the adrenaline of the chase joined by the adrenaline of anticipation.

In a way, this crisis was a relief: there was no question of what she should do, and Parthenon threw herself at it with a will.

Events passed before Alister's eyes like the images of a video on fast-forward: jumping and jerking from one scene to the next, sometimes with large chunks of time missing in between.

They were sliding through the darkness. They were stopped. Someone put a rope in his hand and said "Hold fast to this . . . "

He was pulled along by the rope, crawling on all fours with small, warm, strong bodies on either side of his head. His hands and knees were so cold he could not feel the pain in them, though he knew it was there.

Then they were stopped. Someone said:

"Tau, Vec, get me some eyes."

A little while later, the first Slavic voice said, "Patrol pattern has changed."

"It's going to be tight getting through the orange corridor," said a new voice. They had a jagged, angular accent Alister didn't recognize.

"We'll take the next rotation—and get that chip out of our man, Dostor."

Small hands on Alister again, pulling at his shirt and feeling over the skin on his back. He tried to protest.

"Here, subdermal," said the big Slavic voice. "You might feel a small prick."

Alister wondered what it said about the state of his brain that he didn't feel a thing.

"Good man," said the big voice. "Tau, give me the runner."

Another jerk. The Edinburgh brogue said, "In the hole . . . "

"Positions," snapped the voice that seemed to be in charge.

"On deck . . . "

Movement around him.

"Click one, go," said the brogue, and they were in motion again.

Alister found himself thrust up through a circular hole. There was a corridor beyond lit by dim orange lights. The walls were made of ribby-looking iron, and wouldn't stay still.

They made him walk, somehow, though Alister had to drag himself along the wall. They got to a wall, turned a corner . . .

. . . and he was nearly knocked off his feet by a flood of information from Dave. It was the creature's way of shouting, and it left Alister's inner ears metaphorically ringing.

"Danger, danger," he gasped. "Someone coming . . . danger . . . Dave's says . . . danger . . . "

"We got a terrier," hissed the brogue, and then the dream turned into a nightmare as they were surrounded by people in white encounter suits.

Alister was shoved to the floor. The next thing he knew he was looking up as a fierce battle was fought in the space above him. Rats in silver suits shooting at the humans in white. One of them was caught in a net.

A gloved hand reached for him.

An entirely new sound ripped through the air. It was a sound Alister knew, but from a world so long ago and far away it felt like it was from another life. Yet he knew it, knew it with every fiber of his being, and in the shocking rush of joy and relief that coursed through him he began to laugh.

The hand hesitated.

And the howl came again.

The rats were joined by dogs. A big one with a flying mane of white hair tackled a human, bringing them to the floor, from which they did not rise. The dog turned, unsheathing a giant knife, and fell on the person holding the netted rat.

Weapons were fired. Someone yelped. Other people growled.

Large, paw-like hands grabbed Alister by the shoulders, lifted him, and began to drag him away.

"*Elevators,*" said a canned voice in his ear. "Level 12!"

"We'll not make it!"

"Oh *yes* we will," said a blessedly familiar, husky voice, and another pair of paws landed on Alister.

He was collapsing into the small, square box of an elevator. It was packed with rats—one still cutting their way out of a net—and dogs on two legs. One of them was golden with alert, triangular ears, and wore a purple jumpsuit.

The elevator stopped. They rushed out, Alister now supported by two large, humanoid dogs. Each wore a headset with a little LCD screen.

Their way was blocked by a dozen or so people in dark encounter suits. One of them was small, lithe, with an aggressive set to her shoulders. She was holding a gun trained on the golden wolf.

"You will surrender," she said, her voice amplified. "Or I will execute you *immediately.*"

Alister felt himself falling. Physically, as the dogs on either side laid him down, and mentally as well. He was falling back into the dark place, into his cell. He was there already, curled in a corner, alone. The rats were gone. The dogs were gone. Dave was . . .

Dave was still wrapped around Alister's head.

He wasn't in his cell. He was on a cold, tile floor. The rats and dogs were all around him, laying down their weapons.

Wait, said Dave.

Alister was confused.

Just wait.

Voices above him. Someone was speaking to Agent Parthenon in a smooth, cultured voice. A dangerous voice. Peering up, one-eyed, Alister saw a tall person in a long, black coat.

Parthenon argued. The person in the black coat spoke soothingly. Eventually she threw her hands up and marched away.

Human hands took Alister, put him on a gurney and strapped him down. He'd lost track of the dogs and rats, but Dave was still with him, telling him . . .

Wait . . .

He was being pushed through hallways with bright yellow lights in the ceiling. They hurt to look at, so he closed his eyes.

He was in darkness. A gentle darkness with a faint, blue glow. Someone was peeling Dave off his head.

Alister struggled and realized he was unbound. But his arms were weak and they only flailed, uselessly.

"Easy there, Mr. Bane," said a deep, northern voice. "Your friend here is in almost as bad a state as yourself. I'm just putting him in some fresh water, and then we'll get you cleaned up."

Shakily, Alister rubbed the slime out of his eyes and blinked up at the figure leaning over him.

A broad-shouldered, dark-haired, dark-skinned woman swam into focus. Her hair was cropped in a no-nonsense cut, and she had kind lines around her eyes.

"*Watson,*" Alister whispered.

"People keep getting my name wrong," the woman sighed. "But considering the circumstances, I suppose you can be forgiven."

Alister managed a weak laugh at that, which exhausted the dregs of his strength, and promptly passed out.

He became aware of the voices before he was aware of anything else. He floated in warm, pleasant darkness, and listened.

"Is he still all there, do you know?"

Elo. That was Elo. The golden wolf in the purple jumpsuit. That had been Elo.

"Too early to say, I'm afraid," said the hearty northern voice. *Watterson,* that had been her name. Not *Watson* . . . Dr. Watterson, who'd scraped him off the pavement in the Professor's home world, when he had been on the run from the . . .

"I have high hopes, considering he was able to remain conscious for as long as he did," said a smooth, cultured, English voice. It was the kind of voice one could imagine performing Shakespeare, or announcing on the radio. It gave Alister shivers, even though it seemed the Detective was on their side this time.

"Yes, but he was stewing in your green friend's juices most of the time," said the big, Slavic voice from earlier, and this confused Alister.

Dave made sense. It was improbable, but it made sense. So did Elo's miraculous appearance. Even the Detective and Dr. Watterson, surprising though their presence was, could be believed.

But the rats? Where did they come from? And there had been other dogs, surely—and *dogs,* not *vroknaär* like Elo.

"Don't you dare blame Dave," he heard Elo snap as he struggled to open his eyes—his lids felt unbelievably heavy. "You'd never have gotten him as far as you did without his help."

"I do not think," the Detective cut in smoothly, "that exposure to Dave's, er, *presence* would make much of a difference either way, considering the mental strain he was already under."

"In any case," said Dr. Watterson, "it's no good speculating; we'll just have to see how he is when he wakes up."

At last Alister got his eyes open. He was lying in a bed with blankets up to his neck. Pressure around his left arm suggested a cuff of some kind, and there were tubes disappearing under the covers leading toward it. Following them up, he saw a bag of clear liquid suspended from what looked like a modified coat hanger.

Fluids, he thought, though his mouth was still dry and tacky.

Beyond the coat hanger the room was dim and hard to make out, except for where a group of people were clustered around a large, wooden desk. He recognized the shape of Elo's shoulders—she had her back to him—and across from her the smooth, dark head of the Detective. Beside him sat Dr. Watterson, and between them, filling in the sides of the desk, were an assortment of rats and three more dogs. Alister didn't recognize any of them, save the big white one who he'd seen tackling a man in a suit earlier. This one was leaning back and appeared to have its right foreleg in a sling.

There was no sign of Dave.

Strangely, this was what that spurred Alister into speaking. He tried to ask where Dave was, but what came out sounded more like: *"Burrvis hay-ve?"*

The crowd around the table surged into motion, all save the Detective who simply lifted his ink-black eyes and looked at Alister with a satisfied expression.

Elo was at his side in an instant, joined shortly by Dr. Watterson, with the rats crowding in curiously between and around them.

"Alister? Alister?" said Elo, nosing at him urgently. "Do you remember me, Alister?"

"Of *course* I remember you," Alister tried to say, but it came out more like, "*Occurth a revembuh ye.*" He curled his lips in frustration. "Needth *water,*" he said, as clearly as he could.

"Drink slowly," said Dr. Watterson, producing a small bottle with a soft, rubber straw.

It was difficult, as Alister discovered he was very thirsty. The fluid got sucked up by his dry mouth as fast as he could suck it in, and he worked his free hand out from under the covers so he could nurse the thing more comfortably.

"Where's *Dave*?" he asked again, once his mouth felt more like a mouth and less like sandpaper with a dead slug in it.

"What? Dave?" said Elo, blinking in surprise. "He's just on the other side of you. Put him in a bucket of water, but he insisted on staying close by."

Rolling his head Alister found that there was indeed a bucket on the other side of his bed, filled to the brim with dark water. A single green tentacle with a delicate yellow tip emerged, formed itself into an equilateral triangle, and then disappeared beneath the surface again.

So Dave was all right. Alister lay back with relief.

"How do you feel?" Elo asked.

"I feel *great,*" said Alister vehemently. Now that he'd watered his parched mouth, he felt better than he had in ages. "I'm just fine."

And promptly went back to sleep.

He slept a lot for a long time. Weeks, it felt like, though it was probably only days. He would wake, drink, and sometimes eat the little yogurts and warm cereal that Dr. Watterson put before him. Elo helped him get out of bed and totter over to the bathroom when he needed to, and the sight of a proper, porcelain toilet nearly made him burst into tears.

"I'm so sorry," Elo said, one time when she was tucking him back into bed. "I had no idea it would be so long for you. We all came as fast as we could."

"It's all right," said Alister, falling back against the pillows with relief. "'m just glad ye *came*." He slept, and if he dreamed, he didn't remember.

After a while, he began spending more time awake. He was able to sit up in bed and eat proper meals, and get to and from the bathroom on his own. The IV drip was taken out, and he got to bathe. Afterward he sat in a comfortable, squashy armchair, and listened as Elo told him some of their story.

The rats, he learned, were the result of a genetic engineering experiment, and came from the same world as the exotrain he had been on when he was kidnapped.

"Our prime member," explained the leader of the rats, who was scruffy and brown with a mangled ear and was called Autoclys, "is the Premier of Amphitrite. All seven of us swore to help Professor Odd in any way we could after she . . . uh . . . well, after she helped us out of a tight spot." He fiddled with the collar of his suit. Alister noticed that the rats, rather like the dogs, spoke through little microphones—in the rats' case, these were incorporated into metal collars that seemed imbedded in their skin. Autoclys had a pleasant, vaguely Bostonian accent, while his second-in-command, Rapsidora (larger and golden-brown) spoke with an even heavier Albian brogue than Alister.

"We were meant for assignments too dangerous for humans," explained a small, white rat who was the owner of the

Edinburgh accent. Her name, it turned out, was Astatrix, and she seemed to be in charge of logistics and planning. "Professor Odd found us working a research satellite in a decaying orbit around Alnitak. We would have all died if she hadn't intervened."

In addition to Autoclys, Rapsidora and Astatrix, there was also Tauclavian (dark brown, and the Slavic voice Alister half remembered), Dostor (by far the largest of the rats; twice the size of Rapsidora and pitch black, he was the deep, Russian voice who had told Alister he was a good man. Apparently, he was their medic), and Vectarine (small and unassuming and light brown, with the jagged, angular accent Alister didn't recognize). Most of her silver suit was covered in straps and holsters for weapons, and he didn't ask what her job was.

The Rats of Alnitak, as they called themselves, had had to come to Alister's world by way of one of the naturally occurring portals in the Denallian Belt, which had taken a good deal of preparation and been incredibly dangerous.

"Don't tell your Professor we did it that way," Astatrix told Alister confidentially. "She'll blow her wig right off. There were safer ways, of course, but the Denallian Belt seemed the fastest.

"It was," said Elo. "You certainly beat us here."

Elo's group, it came out, were the descendants of the dogs they had met on Canary 6. Natalyas Boraznes-Swissgard was the youngest daughter of the medic Ksanos Boraznes from Discovery Intent, while Siimo Sant-Akit was the son of Omu Akit. Both dogs were obviously mixes—Siimo had definite St. Bernard features—while the huge white dog with the injured arm, Bursang Samoy, Alister guessed descended from a Samoyed. She seemed embarrassed to have been injured, and mumbled something about how it was an honor to meet the Good Man.

In addition to Elo, however, there was one familiar face. It greeted Alister when he woke and there was no one but Dave for company, springing into view from where its owner had been curled beside Alister's bed. Keeping watch, he realized.

"Hel*lo* there!" it grinned at him, rusty red and round with perked ears, the LCD display on its comsys making a :D.

Alister would have known that voice anywhere, even though it technically came from a computer.

"Reiji?" he asked.

"Of *course* Reiji!" said Reiji Shibo, his tightly curled tail wagging. "Couldn't trust a wolf to lead this mission all on her own! Knew we needed at least *one* original member from Discovery Intent on Retrieval Bound. Shani would have come, but we needed her on the other side to stabilize the Link, and the rest are too arthritic."

"But they're still alive?" Alister asked.

"Of *course* they're still alive!" said Reiji, rolling his eyes. "It hasn't been *that* long. And Neo Canii's got some ideas about what to do with the arthritis, too. Actually, that's partly why we're here: mostly it's for *you* of course, but if we can hunt down some of the packets our previous teams delivered to the Canary Company, well then, all the better!"

The "Link" which Reiji had so casually mentioned turned out to be the main reason that the rats had beaten the dogs: Elo and the dogs of Neo Canii had built a special ship capable of towing the comet bearing the wormhole into a stable orbit of Earth, which they managed to catch on its outward journey from the sun. Then it was a matter of making a vessel capable of traveling *through* the wormhole to Alister's world, and making sure they would come through at the right place on the other side. Luckily, they'd had someone waiting there, ready to help out.

"It was a fascinating problem," said the Detective, leaning back in a rickety wooden chair and crossing his long legs. "Calibrating the portal with such limited technology, I mean. Infiltrating the Company, pah," he rolled his eyes. "They are, it pains me to say, more paranoid than clever, and more interested in developing weapons from their stolen technology than actually studying what is out there. Disappointing, but easy enough to manipulate." He shrugged.

"Yes," said Alister, uncertainly. "But how did *you* get here?"

"Professor called us, didn't she?"   said Dr. Watterson. "Couldn't say no, not when it was for you."

Alister blinked at her. The woman looked down at her shoes.

"Dr. Watterson has been assisting me in my cases for the past year or so . . . local time, of course." The Detective told Alister, with a small, wry smile. "But I believe she would have come anyway, when she learned you'd managed to get yourself into trouble again."

Alister opened his mouth to protest, and then caught the amusement in the man's dark eyes.

The Detective was *joking* with him. Horribly, but he was trying. Alister shut his mouth, and began to reevaluate the man in front of him.

They never said exactly how they managed the jump across worlds, and neither did Dave—though no one bothered to ask. Dave, it seemed, had been obliged to leave his panvironment suit behind, but the rats managed to construct a slime-to-audio translator which, though it was accurate enough, sounded even worse than the last one.

"WOULD YOU PREFER I USE YOUR HEAD?" Dave asked, when Alister remarked on this.

Alister fell silent. He did not like to think about the time when his mind and Dave's had been so closely linked. The way it had opened doors to places beyond his comprehension made him feel dizzy. At the same time, it had given him no lasting trouble. Certainly nothing compared to the confinement and sensory deprivation he'd suffered at the hands of the Canary Company.

Which, it turned out, they had not entirely escaped. Yet.

"Technically we are still within their headquarters," said the Detective, knitting his fingers together. "However, as those are bloated and sprawling, they provide exceptional hiding places, and this way we remain close to the Link, through which we will evacuate our happy band, once Dr. Watterson deems you strong enough to make the jump."

The Link, Alister eventually found out, was the Company side of the wormhole through which the dogs of Reiji's world had been sending information, technology, and—horrifically— *other dogs* for several years. It had a rudimentary set of controls that allowed it to be harmonized with other universes that contained compatible wormholes. It was nothing compared to the Oddity, however, and Elo explained it would be like jumping blind if you didn't have someone on the other side to manipulate the receiving end.

"That's part of why Ksanos had to stay behind," she said. "She's become something of an expert on portals."

The reason they had to wait for Alister to recover was not because going through the wormhole itself was particularly traumatic—that took no time at all—but because they had to do it in a tiny ship that would then plummet to the surface of the planet, with all the associated physical strain.

The rats would join them, even though they had come from the natural portal to the Denallian Belt. This opened in high orbit around Earth as well, and though their ship was capable of making launch, it had been difficult enough landing without being noticed. They doubted a rocket taking off would go un-detected.

This was explained to Alister briskly, cheerfully, as if it were not the maddest idea he'd ever heard. To get to the Link at all they'd have to sneak through the heart of the Canary Company, and though the Detective seemed confident this was possible, Alister doubted it would be so easy.

He'd been having ideas, so strange he could not have voiced them, but they lodged in his heart and grew. Then, on the first day when he was strong enough to get up and do things on his own, he was invited to sit at the large desk as they went over their grand plan of escape. The Detective had barely begun when Alister cut him off.

All he said was, "No," but it caused the entire room—humans and dogs, *vroknaär* and Dave—to go silent.

No one interrupted the Detective, except for Dave, who in-terrupted everyone. The rats respected him grudgingly as a peer of the Professor. The dogs because he was a human. Even Elo and Dr. Watterson let him say his piece before contradicting him.

Now all the eyes at the table turned to Alister, who was sitting across from the Detective, leaning back in his chair. Though he was aware of their combined gaze he felt no pressure or fear of judgment. A dead certainty had settled in his stomach, weighing down the doubts, and with them most of his fears as well. He had always been afraid of not knowing what to do. Now he knew what he had to do, and more importantly, he knew it could be done.

"No," he said again, shaking his head. "We can't leave, not yet."

"Pray, why not?" asked the Detective. His voice was sweet but his eyes were hard. He leaned forward, resting his elbows on the table, and laced his fingers together.

Alister was not intimidated, but he did hesitate.

During his escape he'd been so addled that he'd lost track of time, and even the things he remembered had been divorced from meaning. He'd seen *Elo* and not immediately recognized her.

Now, however, he was beginning to remember meanings without the images to go along with them.

There had been a girl. No, a *woman*. She had a kind face and she'd let him out. She'd been frightened of him, but she'd let him out. *Rajinder* was her name, he remembered because Dave had told him, and he remembered everything Dave had said like a tingle in his brain.

At the time he'd only been aware of the events as they were happening, and everything else had been pushed to the background. Now he realized he'd left a kind, compassionate person in a place where her act of heroism was more likely to be punished—and punished horribly—than rewarded.

She'd not only let a specimen escape, she'd come into contact with *Dave*. And if simply stepping outside the universe was enough to get them interested in Alister, what would contact with Dave entail?

No, Alister couldn't leave things as they were. Not with Rajinder possibly suffering a torture as bad as his own. Not with the Canary Company as it was: a huge, inhumane organization that spread its disruption across multiple worlds. Not when it would chase him—now more fiercely than ever—for the rest of his life.

Something the Professor had said came back to him in meaning and intent, though he could no longer remember the exact words. It made him smile, though, because he knew now how to explain himself.

"You remember how we came back?" he asked the Detective. "That time you were hunting the Professor? After we'd got clean away from you, remember how we came back?"

"I could not forget even if I wished to," said the Detective with a sigh.

Alister nodded. "The Professor said it was the only thing to do. Because otherwise you'd just keep chasing us. So she had to go back and explain."

"Alister," said Elo, and the warning tone in her voice told him she knew what he was thinking. It didn't faze him.

"Well," he forged on. "This is like that. Only bigger. Even more important, because the Canary Company has been making life miserable for a lot of people, across a lot of different worlds."

"What are you steering for, Mr. Bane?" asked Autoclys, his whiskers twitching.

Alister looked around the table and said, quite simply: "We're not running away. We're going to take the Canary Company apart, and *then* we'll leave."

"Are you *mad?*" Elo barked, but Alister saw how Reiji perked his ears, how Rapsidora and Tauclavian looked at him almost hopefully, and how the Detective got an expression of surprised respect on his face.

"Yes," he said, mildly. "I am a little angry. *Listen,* Elo. The Canary Company's been stealing from other worlds—things and knowledge and *people*—for who knows *how long.* And what are they doing? Turning their knowledge into weapons. They're not just getting ready for this universe to become multiplicity-aware—they're getting ready to take it to *war.*"

"Yes, I *know,*" said Elo, pinning her ears back. "But here? Now? We are not *prepared!*"

"Aren't we?" said Alister, looking around at the table. "Because it seems to me we've got *two* crack strike teams, the cleverest, most dangerous man I've ever met, a *very* good doctor"—Dr. Watterson snorted but did not interrupt—"*you,*" he jabbed a finger at Elo, "and *Dave,* and we're *already inside.* I'd say if anyone can do it, *we* can."

He sat back, folded his arms, and looked defiantly around the table. A small acorn of terror had lodged itself in his dead certainty, but this was squashed when he saw the way the Detective was smiling at him.

It was Natalyas who spoke first, her clear, comsys voice cutting into the silence like a sword.

"I did always wonder what happened to Discovery Intent's predecessors," she said, her mouth curling into a slight snarl.

"Never liked bullies, of any species," said Autoclys, and all the rats nodded.

"I do not customarily accept a new commission on top of one not yet completed," said the Detective with a shrug. "But I suppose in this case we may consider it an *extension.*"

"Oh for—" Elo threw up her paws. "Alister, this is *not* what the Professor sent us to do!"

"The Professor sent you all to rescue me," Alister said. "Which you *did.* Thanks. And this is what I think we should do, because it needs to be done, and we've got a chance to do it."

Elo gave him an exasperated look, but Alister was only halfway paying attention. Dave had slipped a single, cool tentacle over his hand, and he felt the word appear soundlessly in the back of his head, giving him all the assurance he would ever need.

Yes.

For Rajinder Ayoadé the following two weeks were the most upsetting she'd ever had—including the bad spell after she and Damien had broken up and the time her cat had gone missing.

It turned out the specimen she'd let out had been of even higher priority than she first imagined, and far from getting fired—though she was certain that was just a matter of time—she was given interview after interview. These culminated with an actual agent coming down from Acquisitions to put her through the meta-scan, which was a machine that was said to be able to read your mind. It gave Rajinder a headache, and the uncomfortable feeling that they had not got what they wanted from her. This was borne out by the fact that she was not allowed to go home, but was escorted to "guest quarters" just a floor above the hi-sec animal ward. Rajinder knew she was essentially a prisoner, and worried herself to sleep every night over what her fate would be.

There had been whispers about what the Company did about security breaches, internal leaks, or plain old incompetence. Rajinder had always been low enough on the food chain she'd thought herself below such punishments, yet now the possibility of being "stripped" and tossed back into the world without a penny or a memory to her name—if they bothered to give her a new one—was a distinct possibility.

Rajinder lay in bed, her mind running circles around all the terrible possibilities her future held, when she heard a skittering from the ceiling, and the light fixture above her bed began to unscrew itself.

She watched it curiously, wondering if she'd gone mad. Then something small and metallic was lowered on a thin piece of wire, until it hung at what would have been eye level if she stood up.

"Well, go on, *take* it," said an annoyed Russian voice.

Automatically Rajinder glanced around to see if she was in view of the surveillance cameras. She couldn't see any, but she assumed she was. Privacy was something only the Director of the Canary Company could afford. (No one had seen him in years: Rajinder thought he must be using up all the privacy allowed in their area, which was why no one else had any.)

"I haven't got all day," said the voice, and the small, metallic thing—which looked a bit like an earplug—began to retreat toward the ceiling.

Rajinder pushed herself up off the bed and snatched it off the wire with a small *pop*.

"Now what?" she asked the light fixture. It wobbled, as if being screwed back into position.

"Put it in your ear," came the voice, now rather muffled. "Do what the good man says."

It sounded a little sarcastic, but Rajinder obediently put the little bud into her ear, where it settled comfortably. She was aware of a faint hum of static, and then a familiar, Albian voice said:

"Hello . . . *am* . . . Rajinder?"

"That's me," said Rajinder, her heart pounding in her chest.

"Right. Good," said the voice. "Okay, give us a wee moment, Rajinder, and we'll have you out in no time. Are you wearing sensible shoes?"

"I—what?" said Rajinder.

"Sensible shoes," repeated the voice, patiently.   "And trousers, preferably. You might have to do a spot of running."

Rajinder looked down at her Company-issued canvas trousers and thick, leather boots which she hadn't bothered to take off.

"Yes," she said, still uncertain.

"Good," said the voice in her ear. Then it went on, apparently speaking to someone else. "I have contact. Let's blow those comm lines."

Agent Parthenon sat in her office, replaying the reel from the Junior Tech's meta-scan over and over again. It didn't tell them much they hadn't already been able to guess, or see from the security cams: Ayoadé had clearly been the victim of a chemical attack and had been coerced into opening the door. How she had gotten the release code was still a mystery, but Parthenon suspected it had something to do with Incongruity M87, which had inexplicably accompanied Specimen 1017 when he exited the cell.

Parthenon chewed on the end of her braid. It was moot now. Agent Barrow had taken them into custody, and from what she knew of the man, she didn't envy them. Far from it.

The truth was, Agent Parthenon kept replaying the reel purely because it was the most recent recorded images she had of Alister Bane.

Alister Bane, who was strong and weak at the same time. Who broke, but cleanly. Who was, when you peeled back his extraordinary history, just a plain, decent young man thrust into a situation far beyond his grasp. Who had made a spirited if ill-thought-out attempt at escape, only to be recaptured.

Agent Parthenon had not been permitted updates on his status since he'd passed out of her jurisdiction, but her thoughts kept going back to him, and with these thoughts her feeling of uneasiness grew.

The Canary Company was necessary. It did good work. It did not make mistakes.

Then what was Alister Bane? Was the fault with Parthenon? No, she had performed her duties perfectly. The fault lay further back, further up, with the person who had first labeled Alister Bane as Specimen 1017, High Priority Asset.

Agent Parthenon shut off the reel and stood up. She left her office and got on the lift up to Administration. She didn't make an appointment. Making an appointment would give her a chance to change her mind. Better to do it now, and get it over with.

Whatever else could be said of her, Agent Parthenon faced her problems head on with all guns blazing.

Two minutes after Rajinder put in the earbud her door sprang open a crack.

"You're clear," said the voice in her ear. "Go through it. Turn left."

Rajinder did so, and was just past the lifts when one of them chimed arrival.

"Corridor on your right, take it," came the instructions, and Rajinder darted down the indicated passage. She'd barely gone ten feet, however, when she ran into a locked door.

"Be ready to enter the combination," said the voice in her ear. "Do you have access to the control pad?"

"Yes," said Rajinder. "But it's bio-locked."

"Bio-locks are overridden. You just need the command code. Ready?"

Rajinder's fingers hovered over the glowing panel. Behind her, she could hear a pair of custodians getting out of the lift. They were speaking together, but quietly.

"Yes," she whispered.

The voice in her ear gave it to her, and she entered it as quickly as she could. The door *dinged* happily, and slid open.

It revealed a tall, brown-haired, pale man with a gaunt, bony face and a close-cropped beard. His hair was a dark fuzz covering his head, and his eyes had not lost the wide, haunted look. He was just in the act of removing a small, silver earbud—the mate of the one Rajinder still wore—and slipping it into the pocket of the neat, black shirt he was now wearing.

There was a shout from behind her.

The man leaned forward, took her lax hand, pulled Rajinder through the door, and slammed it shut behind her.

"Hallo," he said, not letting go of her hand. "Gotta run now."

They did. Down the hall, around a corner, and through another door that sprang open at their approach. It led to a maintenance-access stairwell, and together they started climbing. Despite huffing like a steam train, Rajinder couldn't stop the flow of questions that streamed out of her.

"Who are you—really?"

"I'm just a bloke—*really*," the man replied, tugging her around a landing. "My name is Alister Galross Bane, I'm from Lochgalrosshead, Alba, and this has all been a huge mistake."

"What are you doing *now*?"

"We're trying to stop them making any more mistakes."

By "them" Rajinder assumed he meant the Company, but that didn't explain who he meant by . . .

"Who is *we?*" she demanded.

"Me, the rats—they've infiltrated security control—the dogs, Elo, and the Detective and Dr. Watterson, of course. Oh, and Dave!"

He cut himself off, as if listening to some unheard voice. Rajinder guessed he had another bud in his other ear, because a moment later he cursed, and said—to apparently no one— "What do you *mean* Dave's vanished?"

A short beat.

"Well, did he get the bloody thing shut off?"

Another beat. The man Bane groaned.

"Best thing to do is finish it quickly, then—I'm halfway to Rajinder's extraction point, where is Retrieval Bound with the Director's office?"

They had slowed their climb as they spoke, and were almost at a sedate walk. But Bane's hand was like a metal clamp on Rajinder's wrist, and his eyes darted about the stairwell, so wide the whites showed all around the dark brown irises.

Below them a door banged open. There was shouting.

"South stairs are compromised," he informed his unseen allies. "I'm aborting the climb. I can make it to Retrieval Bound if you open the blue passage. Just *do* it Tauclavian—*now!*"

They reached another landing while the man spoke, and the door out of the stairwell sprang open for them. It revealed a passage that Rajinder had never seen before in person, but she knew it from studying surveillance footage when she was in training.

They were in the upper levels of the Company's main tower, where the senior agents and the Director himself kept their offices. They were pelting along a corridor lit by actual daylight from actual windows. They came to an intersection, where the man turned left and continued running.

"Meant to get you out, first," he panted as they ran. "Sorry 'bout the detour. But I figure safest place for you is probably with the dogs. They'll take care of you while the Detective and I deal with the Director."

A door along the corridor banged open at their approach, and a long, furry arm reached out. Alister grabbed its paw-like hand and swung them both through the door, where they nearly collided with an almost human-sized dog with a bushy, white mane, holding something that looked like a submachine gun slung under one arm.

Here, at last, they stopped, and Rajinder had to double over panting, but she still managed to stare at the people who filled the room.

They were, she was certain, *people*. Even if they looked like dogs. They walked on their hind legs, their feet flat on the ground, with square shoulders and fingers on their hands. Their faces were completely canine, but they all wore headsets with microphones and liquid-crystal displays perched over one cheek.

There were four of them: the big white one, a smaller red-dish one, a jowly tan one, and a slender white-and-cream dog with a narrow, knifelike face. And there was a fifth one who walked on her toes, who did not wear a headset, and whose fur was a brilliant gold. Something about the keenness of her face and the length of her ears suggested *wolf* rather than dog, but Rajinder had no time to ponder the details. An agent walked into the room at that point, followed by a burly woman in a neat, tweed suit.

"What happened?" the man Bane asked, letting go of Rajinder at last.

"Who is *this?*" asked the agent—who, Rajinder began to realize, probably wasn't *actually* an agent. Even if he *was* wearing the Company uniform, all black with a silver badge, and a cold, cruel expression.

"This is Raji—Rajinder," said Bane. "The one who let us out. What *happened?*"

The man who was not an agent shrugged. "Dave infiltrated Defense, and was about to start work on their exterior manipulator, when he abruptly cut contact with us and vanished. I can assure you he was *not* captured, but other than that, he could be anywhere."

The man Bane sighed heavily. "Where are we with the director's door?" he asked.

"Ninety-percent cracked," came a voice from near the floor, and Rajinder blinked down at the largest rat she'd ever seen. A rat in a silver jumpsuit with an assortment of bladed weapons strapped to its back, and a peculiar tablet clutched in its paws. "This would be going faster if I didn't have to keep him from noticing. Do we really have to surprise him? At this point?"

Bane pursed his lips. "Yes," he said, grimly.

They were picking the lock on the Director's inner office door, Rajinder realized, stunned. The not-agent came and stood to one side of the door, while the man Bane took up position opposite him. The golden wolf came and crouched by his elbow, while the burly woman in the tweed suit stood behind the not-agent. She had a small, silver pistol, pointed resolutely at the floor.

"You might want to have a seat over here," said a pleasant, clear voice at her shoulder. Rajinder jerked around to find the pale dog with the narrow face looking at her earnestly. She let it guide her over to the secretary's desk, where the dog briskly picked up the chair that had been knocked over, and settled Rajinder into it.

From where she sat she had a good view of the outer door— the dogs had set up a sort of barricade in front of it and taken up defensible positions behind overturned cabinets and chairs— but she had to crane her neck around to see the door to the inner office, and so she heard more than saw what happened next.

The little rat by the floor said: "Got it. Any time now, gents."

The not-agent looked across at the man Bane, at the gold wolf, and finally over his shoulder at the burly woman with the gun. He nodded once.

"All right then," said the rat, hitting a button on her tablet. "Have at 'em!"

There was a faint *pop* and the door jerked open a crack. The not-agent reached out and pulled it open the rest of the way, just in time for the golden wolf to dive inside, out of sight. It was followed closely by the not-agent, the burly woman, and finally the man Bane.

There were raised voices inside. Rajinder heard the Director's voice—higher and squeakier than it had sounded in public announcements—shouting for someone named Parthenon to *do* something.

Bane gave a startled shout, quickly cut off.   The wolf growled. There was a quiet exchange of voices, a muffled struggle, and then the hiss of a door opening and closing. After that there was silence, and Rajinder heard a deep, northern voice say, quite distinctly:

"Bloody *hell.*"

Parthenon's mind was a blank slate, wiped clean of everything but the sudden need for action. The situation still seemed surreal to her, even as she felt the man's neck under her hand, the weight of his body pressing into the muzzle of her gun, the drag of his feet as she walked him backward into the Director's bolt-hole.

It had been dreamlike, gaining entrance to the inner office, seeing the Director face to face, and then *arguing* with him of all things. Agent Parthenon had never, in all her years of service, ever imagined disagreeing with the Director, let alone taking him to task over a difference of opinion. Yet this she had done, and done with a glad agony, like the lancing of an infected wound, and then . . .

. . . then the door had burst open, and in the manner of dreams there was Specimen 1017—along with Agent Barrow and his assistant, and the golden wolf from the train.

She'd heard the Director's commands only distantly, for her mind had already assessed the situation and her body was taking action.

Specimen 1017 was the most physically vulnerable, so she'd gone straight for him. Got him in a choke hold and used him as a living shield while the Director opened the door to his bolt-hole, dragged him in after him, and only when the door was sealed did she reassess her actions.

The bolt-hole was small, but well fortified—an oblong room with a bunk and a control station, a ration cabinet, a first-aid cupboard, and a small shower stall. Clearly, it was prepared for long-term use, but only by a single individual. The three of them would not be able to remain here for long.

The Director was raving, pulling at his short, curly, black hair. Shouting something about traitors and the Professor. The *Professor,* he was certain, was behind all of this.

"Oh *sure,*" said Specimen 1017, dryly. "*Now* you ask about the Professor."

Director Carver looked like his eyes were going to pop out of his head, he was so furious and frightened.

"Of *course* the Professor!" he practically screamed. "That's why we're interested in *you,* of course! You're the only one we've got that has had prolonged contact with her!"

"Really?" said Specimen 1017. He sounded unimpressed. "I thought you wanted to know about me nonexistent extra-universal travels as a child!"

Parthenon let the conversation wash over her. The blank slate of her mind was filling with urgent thoughts, all jostling for position, all demanding her attention.

Wanting Specimen 1017 for his contact with Specimen 1016 was understandable, but it did not explain why he'd been listed as *partially* human at the very beginning. The only reason that Parthenon could see, if he had not, in fact, been a multiversal traveler at the time, was that listing him as partially human would have made it easier to process him for archival.

And if he had *not* been a multiversal traveler at the time, it meant that the Canary Company, the guard dog of her world, had turned on one of its own.

Agent Parthenon had done a number of things, she knew, that were not entirely nice, all in the name of the Canary Company, with the understanding that everything the Company did was for the benefit of its home world. To protect the innocents still living under the assumption that their universe was the only one, safe and unassailable from the vast multiplicity.

Of which, she felt now with creeping certainty, Specimen 1017—*Alister Galross Bane*—had been.

Her hand tightened unthinkingly on his neck, and the man broke off what he had been saying with a cough.

"I am going to ask you one more time," she whispered in his ear, ignoring the Director, who was practically steaming. "What were your extra-universal travels prior to meeting Specimen 1016?"

Alister Bane rolled his eyes around and glared at her. His face took on a resigned expression, and he said, in a bland, dead tone:

"Once, I found a magic door that led to a planet with huge dandelion flowers, only instead of seeds they had these moths that flew off and pollinated the other plants. *There.* Happy now?"

Agent Parthenon didn't move. Her body felt frozen, her mind like a river rushing beneath a frozen surface, as she stared at his face in horror.

Agent Parthenon could read a person well enough to know when they were lying, provided she had references to work from. It had been difficult to read Alister Bane on account of the fact that she hadn't been able to catch him in a flat-out lie. And now she knew why: up until that moment, everything he'd said had been the truth.

This new bit about going to a planet with giant dandelion flowers, *that* was as plain a lie as Parthenon could ever hope to see.

And if everything else he'd said had been the truth . . .

In the distance she could hear the Director shouting, but he—and whatever he was saying—suddenly seemed unimportant. What was important was the man currently trembling under her grip, brave and frightened and weak and strong all at once. One of theirs. One of *hers.* One of the people she'd signed on to *protect.*

"I am *not* a villain," she hissed at him through gritted teeth, whether for the man's benefit or her own she was uncertain.

Alister Bane dared turn his head to gaze back at her, anguished and sad and so *disappointed* it made Parthenon furious.

"Then stop *acting* like one," he whispered. He sounded more annoyed than anything else.

It was really as simple as that, Parthenon realized with a mix of relief and horror.

The ice inside her mind broke, and thoughts and feelings came pouring through. It shook her, and she ripped her hands from the man, pushing him away while she tried to grapple with the sudden surge of emotions.

Director Carver was shouting at her, and reluctantly Parthenon spared enough attention to translate the noise into words.

"*Parthenon!*" he bellowed, "I *told* you to terminate Specimen 1017! He's more trouble than he'll ever be worth!"

Parthenon froze, anger and betrayal and despair warring with her cold training, leaving her suspended. In that instant she was neither Agent Parthenon nor the girl who had signed up to be a superhero so many years ago. She was a complicated tangle of history and feelings blown sky high and now falling, tumbling, toward a new person she wasn't quite sure of yet.

She felt the impact of the projectile before she felt the pain. It nearly knocked her leg out from under her, and she staggered, just as another hit her square in the stomach. The next thing she knew she was on the ground, her entire lower half alive with pain, and worse, the particular knowledge that an artery had been lacerated. She stared blankly at the Director, who was re-aiming the hand rifle he'd pulled from the rations cabinet so that the muzzle was pointed straight at her head.

Wait, Parthenon thought. *I'm not me yet . . .*

It was a strange feeling, going from having a gun pressed into his spine, to seeing the owner of said gun getting shot. There was no explosion of blood or flesh, just the loud *bang* of the weapon firing, and then Agent Parthenon was staggering. Another *bang* and she doubled over, collapsing to the floor. Alister could only stare in mute horror when the blood finally came, pouring alarmingly from the wound in her left leg.

Only when he saw the Director raising his gun a third time was he able to act, and then it seemed only natural to charge at the man, grab his gun hand and turn it to the wall, sending the third shot into the first-aid cupboard—which was a grotesque sort of irony, Alister thought—and try to wrestle it from his grasp.

Neither of them were trained fighters, that much was clear, and Alister had the advantage of height. The Director still held the gun, however, and it went off twice more while Alister tried to twist it out of his grip. It was a miracle neither of them were hit.

Then, in the sudden way things seemed to be happening, the man went limp in Alister's arms, and he looked up to find himself nose to nose with Agent Parthenon, her dusky face gone greenish and stretched with pain, and then the three of them were slowly crumpling to the floor, collapsing in a messy pile of limbs and blood.

At last Alister managed to wrench the small, evil rifle away from the Director, and he threw it blindly across the floor.

There was no need. The man—the neat, dark-skinned man who had once led him through the bowels of the Canary Company, into an office not unlike this one—lay limp and motionless under him. Even before Alister could check for breath or pulse he knew he must be dead: there was a mean, thick knife sticking out the back of his neck near the base of his skull, and Parthenon's gloved hand still clung weakly to the handle.

The woman lay back against the floor, and though she still breathed, it was with quick, shallow breaths, and her lips had gone bluish.

Alister tried to get up, and nearly slipped in the puddle of blood that had spread under them even in that short time. So he shoved the late Director aside and crawled over Parthenon, feeling clumsily for the wound in her leg, which seemed to be the source of the blood.

"I'm sorry," he found himself saying, for lack of anything better. "I'm sorry. I'm sorry." Sorry for not knowing how to stop the bleeding. Sorry for not being able to take a gun away from a crazy man. Sorry for . . . well, sorry for getting her shot, really.

S'all . . . s'all right," said Parthenon, her voice weak and slurred. She batted limply at Alister's shoulder. "Don't . . . don't bother."

"I have medics on my team," Alister said. "One of 'em's a really good doctor. She'll patch you up no problem. Let me put something on this, they'll get that door open in no time."

He crawled around, trying to reach the first-aid cupboard while still keeping pressure on the leg wound, and found he couldn't reach. He paused, momentarily stumped, and Parthenon gave him a pained smile.

"You're a good man, Mr. Bane," she said, unsticking her mouth with visible effort. "Anyone ever tell you that?"

Reluctantly Alister crawled back over to her and placed both hands on the leg wound. Blood kept seeping up through his fingers, but he tried not to think about it.

"They might have mentioned it, yeah," he said.

Parthenon blinked at him, her eyes coming briefly into focus. They were a remarkable tint of hazel, Alister realized. He'd never noticed before.

"You've gotta . . . gotta promise me something," said the bleeding woman, clearly fighting to stay conscious.

"Aye?" said Alister, figuring he probably owed it to her.

"Take care . . . take care of the Company," she said, regarding him with dim gravity.

"Sorry?" said Alister, certain he hadn't heard right.

"S'important, what we do. What we've been *s'posed* to be doing. Guard dog. Watch dog. Like Cerberus. Canary Company, like *canii*, like dogs. Important that . . . that we're here. Big multiverse. Not friendly."

"Not all of it," Alister protested.

"People here need looking after," Parthenon went on, ignoring him. "You got to look after my boys. Caruthers, Villafranka. Can't let people like Carver lead them. They go . . . go wrong in the head. Wrong like me. Lose themselves."

"That's not what I—" Alister began, and then stopped. Agent Parthenon's eyes had unfocused. How long would it take Vectarine to unlock the reinforced door?

"Okay," Alister said, gratified when Parthenon seemed to focus on him. "Okay, I'll . . . I'll look after them. I'll take care of it. All of it."

Parthenon smiled blearily at him.

"Know you can do it," she said, letting her head fall back. "Know you can . . . the Professor . . . she taught you things. Taught you good."

"Aye," said Alister, sliding himself up so he could keep eye contact, but Parthenon had shut hers. "Parthenon?" he tried.

A flutter. A flash of hazel.

"Name's Octavia," the woman mumbled.

"Octavia? Please, you've got to stay awake."

Octavia Parthenon blinked up at him and frowned. "I'm sorry, Mr. Bane," she whispered. "Tell her . . . tell her I wish

we could have met . . . in a different life. Different circum . . .
stances . . . "

"Well, it is an infinite multiverse," Alister said with forced
cheer. "Perhaps, in some other time and place, you will."

"That'll be . . . nice," said Octavia Parthenon, her eyes drifting shut and her face going lax. And though Alister called her
name, shouted, even gently shook her shoulders, she never
opened them again. Her breath slowed to a gurgling hiss, so
faint that when the door came open at last (with a small *bang*:
Vectarine had had to resort to slightly more violent methods)
and Dr. Watterson hurried inside, the first thing she did was
put on a plastic mask and breathe into the unconscious agent's
mouth. She handed one to the Detective, who took over al-
ternately blowing air into Parthenon and pressing firmly on her
chest, while Dr. Watterson inspected the leg wound. At the look
on her face, Alister knew it was all over. Still, they called in Dostor, and between the three of them they worked for another fifteen minutes, before Dostor sat back on his haunches and shook
his head.

"We are literally beating a dead human," he announced.
"Call it."

"Who was she?" Dr. Watterson asked Alister, tired and concerned.

Alister could only shrug.   "Her name was Octavia
Parthenon," he said. "Beyond that, I'm not really sure."

He got up and walked over to the control console. It was
bio-locked, but a little help from Dr. Carver's body soon had him
accessing all the man's files—and the communication system for
the entire Company's complex.

"Security," he said, and was gratified when he heard Tauclavian's voice respond immediately.

"Don't scare me like that, Bane!"

"How are things with you?"

"All good and quiet over here. Still in control. But Vec says you had some excitement?"

"You could say that," said Alister. "Look, do me a favor, I'm going to make a Company-wide announcement. Can you, like, do a little something, make sure everyone's listening?"

"*Da, da*," said the rat. "Easy."

"Mr. Bane," said the Detective, looming over Alister's should like a tall, disapproving shadow. "What are you doing?"

Alister pursed his lips, took a deep breath, and squared his shoulders. "The right thing, I hope," he said.

Crouched under the secretary's desk, Rajinder was surprised when she heard the musical cue signaling a public announcement. It surprised the dogs, too, who had temporarily relaxed when Elo reported that Alister was alive and unharmed, and that Carver was dead.

Rajinder was still reeling from that, even though she had no love for the man, when a voice that was not the Director's spoke where before only the Director's had been heard.

"*Employees of the Canary Company,*" it said. "*This is your director speaking. I would like to apologize for any disruption our recent security exercise might have caused in your work. You will be glad to hear that it was a success, and things will now return to normal. However, in the coming days I plan to execute a complete overhaul of this company, to better facilitate our ultimate mission: to protect our universe. Please use this time of change to reassess your own goals and work habits, as we work together to right old wrongs, and clean out the corners which have become unfortunately cluttered with unnecessary projects. Thank you."*

Alister leaned back from the microphone and let out a deep breath. His hands were shaking, but there was a lightness in his chest, and a certainty in his gut, that told him he was doing the right thing. Then there was a weight on his shoulder, and he looked up to find the Detective gazing down at him.

"Well done, Mr. Bane," he said quietly. "Well done, indeed."

Alister rubbed the fuzz on the back of his head. "I hope so," he said.

There was a startled gasp, and they both looked around to find the woman, Rajinder, peering in at the mayhem and gore with a look of horror on her face.

"Sorry about the mess," said Alister, and her eyes jerked toward him. "You're not in any trouble, though. In fact," he added, with a burst of inspiration. "Would you like a job?"

It was a frighteningly easy process, taking over the Canary Company. The Director had become so much of a recluse in the time since Alister and Professor Odd had made their improbable escape—which had been *five years* of native time, Alister was stunned to discover—that it was possible for Alister, who neither looked nor sounded like the late man, to slip into his shoes with only a modest amount of deception. Tauclavian set up a voice filter for him that made him sound like Dr. Carver when he made his company-wide announcements, and for everything else he needed done in person he sent the Detective, whose false identity as Agent Barrow turned out to be invaluable. Then it was just a matter of sorting through the frightful mess that the Company had become, pruning off the bad bits—like Dr. Carver's old secretary, who had been absent for the entire confrontation thanks to a little trickery by Astatrix and so could be safely reassigned without having his head meddled with—and promoting good, new growth.

One of the first things Alister did in this regard was make Rajinder his new secretary, though the woman refused that title.

"Call me your Executive Assistant," she said, her dark eyes glittering. "I like that."

It turned out she also liked organizing things even more than Alister, and soon he left her on her own to sort through the Company's rosters. She had, after all, first-hand experience with most of these people and was a better judge of their characters than he.

This left Alister free to settle some pressing unfinished business—namely, what had become of Dave.

The creature had last been heard from on his way to Defense, which was a wing of the Company devoted to extra-universal protection, and where they suspected the machine interfering with the Oddity's portal was located. Dave, it appeared, had found the machine, locked down the room it was in, and then disappeared. When Vectarine finally managed to get the door open the room was deserted save for the machine, which Dave had smeared with slime that said *Do not touch*, and a small puddle of slime in the middle of the floor.

Alister knelt there, in front of the black, button-studded face of the machine, and cautiously dipped a finger in the puddle.

Dave's voice—his real voice—crept into his mind, but faintly. As though he were listening to a recording left on someone's answering machine.

Apologies, Alister. And Odd, when she arrives. I am unable to complete my mission, and it may be a long duration before we see one another again. Unforeseen complications have arisen which require my presence elsewhere. I will find you later. I exist . . .

. . . then there was a complicated bundle of feelings and tastes that Alister could not put into words. He stood up, feeling dizzy and a little heartbroken. He had the slime scooped into a small jar, sealed, and ever after carried it around with him, since Dave obviously meant the Professor to hear it as well.

He was laid surprisingly low by the loss of Dave, even though, as Elo pointed out, *no one* on their team had *actually* died. This was true, Alister realized with a stunned sense of relief. Aside from Bursang's strained shoulder, the dogs of Retrieval Bound had suffered no injuries, and all the rats had come through unscathed. Alister clung to this comforting fact, since the more he delved into the workings of the Company, the more depressing it became. When they found the vault that housed the previous reports and artifacts from the dogs' world, Reiji threw a fit. There, alongside his world's best technology, were the preserved corpses of his predecessors. Many of whom, it was clear, had made it through the portal alive, only to have died as a result of the experiments later performed on them.

Less disturbing, but even more troubling, was what Alister found when he had all the cells in the high-security animal ward opened up: animals from other universes, many of whose species he did not recognize. The Company had kept scrupulous records of where each animal had come from, but since most were in no condition to be sent back, this was of little use to Alister. He had to train up a new batch of techs to care for them properly, while he and the Detective set about recalibrating the Link so that, once rehabilitated, they could each be returned to their respective universe.

One specimen, however, they did not return. They found it in the robotics wing, and Alister immediately set Tauclavian and Vectarine the task of dismantling it and destroying the components. He then had to go and rage at Elo about it.

"An *Antimovian!*" he gasped, burying his face in his hands. "They'd got a bloody *Antimovian* locked up in there! Sure, it was deactivated—*or so they thought*—but really, that's just asking for trouble!"

"This whole place was asking for trouble," said Elo, darkly. She was still angry on the dogs' behalf over what had become of their previous Canary 6 teams.

Some things they found, however, were more amusing than disturbing. Alister went through his own file with a wry grin on his face. Someone—probably Dr. Carver—had worked very hard to make him look a lot more dangerous than he was. There he found both of the folded paper birds he had left for the Company—the one he left in his abandoned dorm room, and the one he'd sent with Discovery Intent's modified package—and these he kept on his desk in the Director's inner office, while the seed of an idea sprouted in his head, cautiously unfurling delicate, new leaves.

The dogs went home after the last of the alien animals had been returned. Alister accompanied them to the Link—which was an arc of metal and wires over a worn concrete slab with a giant red X painted on its surface. He hugged each dog before they climbed into their little space pod—since their side of the portal opened in high orbit around Earth—but Reiji gripped his hands and made him promise to come for a visit.

"You'd be something to show my great-grandpups," he said. "Which is something I'll actually get to do, thanks to all the lost tech we're bringing back."

Alister smiled but made no promises. They retreated a safe distance while Elo activated the Link, and in a flash of blinding light, the ship vanished.

The rats stayed on for almost six whole months after the surprise coup. Alister needed their help running the security system, which controlled every aspect of the physical buildings the Company inhabited. Once he and Rajinder had picked out a trustworthy team of new recruits and got them trained up, however, the rats went home as well. They didn't leave through the Link, but on their own ship, which as Alister now had full control of the Company and could tell the governments of Earth not to mind the rocket they were sending into orbit, they were able to do.

"If we see the Professor, we'll let her know what's happened," Autoclys assured him, and Alister had to be satisfied with that.

To someone working at the Company the shift from militant to scientific, from defense oriented to *study* oriented, came about gradually and, it seemed, naturally. Few people were actually fired, but there was a lot of reorganization of personnel. Many of the operatives found themselves assigned to boring tasks, while many techs got surprise promotions. A lot of the custodians left of their own accord, disappointed in what the Company was becoming but too disheartened to start up again somewhere else. They drifted back into a world that had been kept ignorant of their work, and found themselves under appreciated and unbelieved. Meanwhile, new blood kept flowing in, until the roster of employees at the Company was almost unrecognizable from what it had been a year before.

It was at that time that the Director announced a small cosmetic change. The Company's name remained the same, but their logo got an overhaul. The two Cs stayed, but the three-headed, winged dog was removed, and in its place appeared a small bird, its wings outstretched. In metal it was simple relief, but on the Company stationary, and anywhere else it appeared in color, the bird was bright yellow.

The Detective left shortly after that, along with Dr. Watterson. It was a small relief to see him go, Alister had to admit, even though he would miss the doctor. The Detective was invaluable as an ally, but Alister could never shake the feeling that he was planning something else. That he was altogether *unsafe* to be around. Yet he was perfectly amicable when they said their good-byes, and Alister found himself thanking the man wholeheartedly.

"And, if you see the Professor . . . " Alister began, and trailed off.

"Yes, yes, of course," said the Detective. "I will, of course, relay the glad news. I fancy, however, that the next time my path crosses hers will also be the next time my path crosses *yours.* Good day, Mr. Bane."

Alister watched on the security video as the Detective and Dr. Watterson walked out the front doors of the Company, got into a waiting cab, and drove away.

Then it was just Alister and Elo—and Rajinder, who took over more and more of the day-to-day running of the Company. She and Alister had many long talks about this, while Elo got more and more impatient.

It had *been* a whole *year.* The Professor *should* have turned up by now. But the days crept past, and no magic doors opened. In his heart, Alister began to fear that they never would. Nevertheless he made arrangements that, should any magic doors happen to open, and should a person resembling the since-deleted description of Specimen 1016 come striding into the halls of the Company, all would be ready for her.

Epilogue

Professor Odd looked around the outer office with new appreciation once Alister finished recounting the events of the past two years. She got up. She walked across and bent over Rajinder's desk, squinting at the main monitor. She went to a window and peered out. Then she turned around, clasped her hands behind her back, and inhaled deeply.

"Well," she said, and seemed not to know what to say next.

"*Well,*" she repeated, her forehead creasing.

"We-ell . . . " she said, chewing on her lower lip.

Alister began to feel nervous. He thought he'd matured a lot in the two years since last he'd set eyes on the Professor, but seeing her again—and so clearly *just* as he remembered her—had brought him right back to the exotrain and the moments before everything went to hell. Suddenly, it was dreadfully important that *Professor Odd* thought he'd done the right thing, never mind what anyone else said.

"I know it's not . . . " he began, and had to stop and swallow, nervous as the first time he'd seen her without her wig on. "I know it's probably not what *you'd* have done . . . " he tried.

Professor Odd looked up at him, sharply.

"No," she admitted, and shrugged. "It's not what I'd have done. But you know something, Mister Alister?" Now her face brightened, and she smiled, thin and delicate. "I don't think I could have done any better."

She was grinning wholeheartedly now, and Alister felt himself returning the expression. He stood there, stupidly happy, as she walked over and clapped him on both shoulders. "No," she said, her smile wide and white. "I couldn't have done better myself."

A small kernel of discontent ruptured Alister's balloon of joy. His smile faltered.

"I'm sorry," he said. "About Dave."

Professor Odd shrugged and shook her head. "We'll find him," she said. "Or more likely, *he'll* find *us.*"

"I still have his message," Alister assured her. "If you'd like to . . . am . . . listen to it?"

"Yes," said the Professor, thoughtfully. "Yes I think I should."

Alister produced the jar and handed it to her. While Professor Odd dipped a cautious finger into the viscous liquid Alister went over to Rajinder's station.

"Any word from Elo?" he asked.

"You *know* what sending messages through the Link is like," she hissed at him. "It could be *weeks.*" She glanced at the Professor, her eyes wide.

"So that's . . . ?"

"Yes," said Alister.

"Should I invite her to dinner?"

"I don't know if she'll stay that long," Alister admitted.

Professor Odd was thoughtful as she wiped her finger on the front of her coat and handed the jar back to Alister.

"Keep it," he said. "He meant the message for both of us, and I've got my own copy. I mean, portion. Whatever."

Professor Odd rolled her lips between her teeth and nodded, tucking the jar away inside her coat.

"I've been meaning to ask," Alister said. "What was it he said, there at the end? After the bit about '*I exist . . .* '"

"Hmm?" said the Professor. "Oh, that was sort of a sign-off. Like the way you or I would sign a letter. A multisensual signature, you might say."

"You mean *that* was his name?" Alister sputtered.

Professor Odd grinned at him. "Pretty much. Now you know why I called him Dave."

Alister had to admit she had a point.

In the tentative lull in conversation, while Rajinder looked like she was working up the courage to ask the Professor to join them for a meal, Alister heard the unmistakable sound of claws in the hallway, and a moment later the door burst open for the second time that morning, and Elo exploded into the room.

"*Finally!*" she howled, throwing herself at the Professor, her tail working like a propeller.

"Elo!" Professor Odd cried, flinging her arms wide as she was knocked off her feet by the charging canine.

"That was fast," Alister remarked, surprised and pleased, watching the two collapse into a happy pile at his feet.

"Got your message right before I left," Elo panted, and it was clear she had: she was still wearing her pressurized spacesuit. It must have been uncomfortable for Professor Odd, being pressed against it by the *vroknaär's* embrace, but she was grinning and laughing and stroking Elo's neck. "*Lucky* thing!" she said, her voice an excited yap.

"This whole incident has been a lucky thing," Professor Odd said, raising herself onto her elbows and grinning up at Alister.

He had to laugh, and in that moment, when they were all happily disarmed, Rajinder stood up, straightened her coat, and said:

"Don't you even think of disappearing on us now, Professor. You must stay—at least for dinner." She seemed a little consternated when, far from arguing, Professor Odd agreed at once.

They ordered in—which was standard procedure whenever Elo was around for meals—but gathered in the tree-lined courtyard in the middle of the complex, where many employees went to eat their packed meals. Everyone knew Elo, by this point, and though Professor Odd got a few curious glances, her proximity to Rajinder rendered her safe from any probing questions.

"They don't know who I am," Alister explained quietly, around his plate of curried potatoes. "I mean, ostensibly I'm a friend of Rajinder's who sometimes joins her for meals. They call me Alex. But as far as they know it's still Dr. Carver in the inner office. We decided it was best that way."

"I think he should retire soon, though," said Rajinder, helping herself to another serving of braised carrots.

They ate and chatted; Elo had to tell her portion of the story all over again, and had the Professor fill them in on her actions since last they'd seen one another. Eventually they walked back up to the director's office, but Professor Odd paused, glancing down the hallway that led to the Oddity.

"It seems, Mister Bane, that you have handled things so well here, you hardly have need of me anymore," she said.

Alister rounded on her.

"*What?*" he exclaimed. "After all the time I spent *waiting?* Oh no, Professor Odd. Don't you think about scurrying off—not without *me.*"

Professor Odd blinked at him.

"But," she said. "You only came away in the first place because you were running from the Canary Company." She gestured at the empty hall. "They're not chasing you anymore: *you* took care of that. You can go *home* now."

"Yes, yes, I thought about that," said Alister, waving a hand impatiently. "I even went for a visit to the Old Country. Sent my grandparents into fits, but they're all right. House is still the same. Village still the same. But it's not *home,* not anymore." He looked very hard at the Professor, since it was important he make her understand.

"Look," he said. "Last time I left—the first time—it was because I dinnae have a choice. Well, now I *do* have a choice, and I've decided I'd like to keep traveling with you . . . if that's all right," he added, suddenly uncertain.

But Professor Odd was grinning at him, a huge smile of amazement and disbelief. It gave him the courage to go on.

"And . . . and I feel I owe it to him, to find Dave."

Professor Odd nodded, understanding, but then she frowned.

"You'll need some time, I expect," she said. "To tidy things up here, I mean. You're not just a university student anymore, Mister Bane. You're the director of the Canary Company."

"*Yes,*" admitted Alister. "As to that . . . give us a wee moment?"

He left Professor Odd in the hall and dashed into the Director's office, and then into the inner office, and finally into the bolt-hole. He pulled open the first-aid cupboard, and from that removed the bulky, blue carpet-bag and the slim, black briefcase that he'd kept at the ready for the past eighteen months. On his way out he was stopped by Rajinder, who was twisting her hands nervously together.

"Do you want to read over Dr. Carver's retirement announcement?" she asked.

"I trust you've done a masterful job of it," Alister assured her. He gave her an awkward bow. "Congratulations on another promotion, Director Ayoadé."

Rajinder rolled her eyes at him. "Get out," she said, then added: "But come back occasionally, yeah?"

"Count on it," Alister assured her, and walked out into the hall.

He had half feared that the Professor would have vanished on him, but she was still there, with Elo at her side, looking mildly surprised.

"You *have* given this a good think," she said.

"Eighteen months," Alister said, grinning. "Rajinder and I planned to make the switch ages ago, but then we got stuck, waiting for you."

Professor Odd looked around the hall. She put her hands behind her back and rocked forward on her toes.

"Just one question, Mister Alister," she said. "Why keep the place going at all?"

Alister blinked at her, surprised at how readily the answer sprang to mind.

"Because Parthenon was right," he said. "You can't just snap the head off a thing like the Canary Company. There's enough people here with questionable ethics that they need a good place to work, to keep them from making trouble. And besides, there *really are* things in the multiverse to be afraid of. Killer robots, for example. A world needs someone watching out for things like that. But not a violent guard. Not a Cerberus. It's like what you said when you first learned this was called the *Canary* Company."

"The canary in the coal mine?" Professor Odd asked.

Alister nodded. "Something that can detect a danger before it's a danger. Something to warn people if trouble is coming. And something to work on a solution, if trouble does come. *That's* what this world needs, and that's what the Canary Company is now."

Professor Odd smiled. It was brief, but bright.

"Don't worry, Professor," said Rajinder, leaning on the door to the director's office. She'd grown, if possible, somehow larger all over in the course of the last year. More confident, assured. Even if she was a little starstruck at the moment, she managed to look perfectly calm as she said: "I'll make sure we stay on track. And if there's any trouble, be sure you'll hear from me."

Professor Odd regarded the round, serious woman, and nodded. "Yes," she said. "I expect I will."

"If you've all quite *finished,*" said Elo, putting her paws on her hips. "*I'm* ready to go home. So long, Raji. It's been swell. We'll be back for Christmas."

Rajinder laughed, and walked them down the hall to where the Oddity waited. To Alister it looked like any other door, but when Professor Odd dragged it open there were the familiar, carpeted steps, the salmon wallpaper, and beyond that the dim, colored lights.

"Wow," said Rajinder, peering up at them. "I almost wish I was going with you. Maybe we could spell each other? After you find Dave?"

Alister agreed that this sounded like a fine deal. He hugged Rajinder, said a last, internal good-bye to the halls of the Canary Company, then followed Professor Odd's bright green coat up the steps and back into the Oddity at last.

It was exactly the same, and new all over again. Alister found that he'd remembered some things wrong and forgotten others entirely: like the delicate spiral pattern on the lace curtains, and the particular smell of wood and tea and spices that seemed to come from everywhere and nowhere.

The musical sounds of the Oddity disconnecting from his home world were as familiar as before, and he stretched out with glad relief into the nearest cushy armchair.

"Well, Alister?" said Professor Odd, spinning around in her seat at the cockpit. "After all this, I think you have earned the right to call our next destination."

"Oh please," groaned Elo. "Can't we just *drift* for a while?"

Alister thought he agreed with her, then he thought of something.

"I had a dream once, while I was waiting for you," he said. "At the time it seemed almost like a memory, even though I knew it never happened. There was this world with these huge, dandelion-like flowers. Only instead of fluffy seeds, they had moths. Moth-seeds, you know? And when they bloomed all the moths flew away. I don't suppose you know of a world where that's real?"

Professor Odd shook her head. "Can't say I do," she admitted. Then she perked up. "But then, we do have an almost infinite number of universes left to explore. They might very well exist somewhere . . . out there. *You never know.*"

"But not now," Alister added, hastily. "I want a nap first. *In my own bed.*"

"Seconded," agreed Elo. "Sleep first, then adventures."

And, for the moment, Professor Odd had to be satisfied with that.

THE END

FURTHER READING

This is the twelfth novella of Professor Odd. The next adventure can be found in:

PROFESSOR ODD #13:

THE ANGELS OF TYSON 4

ABOUT THE AUTHOR

Goldeen Ogawa is an author and illustrator of science fiction and fantasy whose works include the *Professor Odd* novellas, *The Adventures of Bouragner Felpz*, the *Driving Arcana* series, and the webcomic *Year of the God-Fox*.

She has been telling stories since before she could read or write and has been drawing pictures the whole time. Her chief inspirations are the natural world, science of all kinds, and frustration with the inherent unfairness of the world in general. She lives in Bend, Oregon, where she rides her bicycle year round.

Her official website is

www.goldeenogawa.com

TEXT AND DESIGN

The body of this book was typeset using $\LaTeX$ in Carter Sans.

Cover art, interior illustrations, and book design by the author.